*Indulge in some perfect romance
from the incomparable*

PENNY JORDAN

**The all new Penny Jordan
large print collection gives you
your favourite glamorous
Penny Jordan stories in
easier-to-read print.**

Penny Jordan has been writing for more than twenty-five years and has an outstanding record: over 165 novels published including the phenomenally successful A PERFECT FAMILY, TO LOVE, HONOUR AND BETRAY, THE PERFECT SINNER and POWER PLAY which hit *The Sunday Times* and *New York Times* bestseller lists. She says she hopes to go on writing until she has passed the 200 mark, and maybe even the 250 mark.

Penny is a member and supporter of both the Romantic Novelists' Association and the Romance Writers of America—two organisations dedicated to providing support for both published and yet-to-be published authors.

MISTRESS OF CONVENIENCE

Penny Jordan

First published in Great Britain 2004
by Mills & Boon, an imprint of Harlequin (UK) Limited,
Large Print edition 2011
Eton House, 18-24 Paradise Road,
Richmond, Surrey TW9 1SR

© Penny Jordan 2004

ISBN: 978 0 263 22332 3

Harlequin (UK) policy is to use papers that are natural,
renewable and recyclable products and made from
wood grown in sustainable forests. The logging and
manufacturing process conform to the legal environmental
regulations of the country of origin.

Printed and bound in Great Britain
by CPI Antony Rowe, Chippenham, Wiltshire

CHAPTER ONE

'Wow, will you look at that? His Royal Highness and the industrialist everyone swears is not up for a knighthood. And don't they look cosy together for two people who are supposed to be sworn enemies.'

As Suzy struggled to hear the voice of Jeff Walker, the photographer from the magazine they both worked for, over the noise of the busy launch party, she heard him saying excitedly, 'I've just got to get a shot of that. Come on.'

This was her first month on the magazine, and immediately she followed him.

She had taken a couple of steps when she heard him saying bitterly, 'Hell! He's got Colonel Lucas James Soames with him. Ex-Commando, Special Forces, hero, and hater of the press!' he explained impatiently when he saw Suzy's uncertain frown. 'Despite the fact that a female reporter with a certain British news team practically dribbled with lust every time she interviewed him during his last campaign.'

Suzy tried to look as though she was up to speed with what she was being told, but the plain truth was that she knew nothing of Colonel Soames. Already unnerved by the photographer's comments, she looked round discreetly, but was unable to spot anyone wearing any kind of military uniform.

She knew she ought to be grateful to her university tutor for recommending her for this job. He had been so enthusiastic about it, telling her what a wonderful opportunity it would be for her, that she had felt she would be letting him down if she didn't accept the probationary position. But after nearly a month working on the political affairs desk of the cutting-edge City magazine Suzy was beginning to suspect that she had made a mistake.

Maybe it was the fact that she had been out of the swim of things for so long whilst she nursed her mother through the last two years of her life that made her so uncomfortable about the methods the magazine adopted in order to get its hot stories. She had certainly felt immeasurably older than her fellow students when she had returned to university to complete her degree.

'I'm sorry—' She began to apologise uncertainly to Jeff. 'I can't see the Colonel.'

But she could see a man several yards away, who stood head and shoulders above every other man in the room—or so it seemed to Suzy. She was transfixed, every female hormone in her body focusing on him with an eager interest. Her mouth had gone dry and her heart had started to pound unevenly. The fact that he was standing alone, somehow aloof from everyone else, only piqued her interest further.

She had the most unexpected and dangerous urge to go up to him and make him... Make him what, exactly? Acknowledge her presence? Talk to her? Tell her that he was experiencing the same heart-wrenching, sanity-undermining, wholly unfamiliar need to be with her that she was experiencing for him? Was she going crazy? Her legs had gone weak and her heart was racing. She didn't know whether it was shock that was running through her body with mercurial speed or excitement. Her? Excited by a man? A stranger? She was too sensible for such stuff. Too sensible and too wary!

Determinedly she started to look away, but he had turned his head, and her heartbeat went into overdrive whilst a surge of explicit and bewildering arousal and longing raced though her. Longing for a man she had only looked at? How could that happen?

And yet Suzy couldn't help watching him. He wasn't looking at her, but past her, she recognised. However, whilst he did so, Suzy was able to stare at him and greedily absorb every tiny physical detail. Tall, dark and handsome went nowhere near describing his full male magnificence. He was more than that. Much, much more! Suzy could feel her whole body responding to just about the sexiest man she had ever seen and was ever likely to see. Her heart gave another small nervous flurry of thuds when he turned his head again, as though he knew that she was now looking at him. He was now staring straight at her, imprisoning her almost, so that she felt unable to move!

She felt as though she was being X-rayed—and that there wasn't a single thing he didn't know about her! Pink-cheeked, she realised that his incisive gaze had finished sweeping her and was now fixed on her mouth. She felt her lips starting to part, as though they were longing for his kiss. Hurriedly she closed them, her face still burning.

His eyes were a shade of intense dark blue, his skin tanned, his hair so dark brown that it was almost black. His profile was that of a Greek god and, as though that wasn't enough, Suzy was forced to acknowledge that he had about him that indefinable air that whispered into the female ear *sex*. And not just any old kind of sex either, but dream-breaking, heart-stopping, mind-blowing wonderful sex! In fact the kind of sex…

Somehow she managed to get her wayward thoughts under control just in time to hear Jeff telling her curtly, 'You're going to have to distract the Colonel's attention whilst I get my picture.'

'What?' Suzy asked, anxiously scanning the crowd packed tightly around the Prince.

'Where…where is he…?'

'Over there—next to the Prince and the Secretary of State.'

Wildly Suzy looked from the photographer's face to the man he had just indicated. *The* man. *Her* man…

'But…but you said he was a colonel. He isn't in uniform.' She was stammering like an idiot—behaving like a woman who had fallen passionately in love! Now she *knew* that she was crazy.

'Uniform?' Jeff's voice was impatient, contemptuous of her ignorance. 'No, of course he isn't in uniform. He isn't in the Army any more. Where have you been? He works on his own, freelance, providing a bespoke protection service for those who need it. Not that he needs to work. He's independently wealthy and well connected; his father was the younger son of an old county family, and his mother was American. He's ex-Eton. Cut his teeth in Northern Ireland and got made up to Major, then was decorated for service above and beyond the call of duty in Bosnia—that's when he got his next promotion. Like I just said, he isn't in the Army any more but he still does the dangerous stuff—acting as a personal bodyguard. He's in great demand on the ''I'm an important person and I need a top-class protection service'' circuit. Visiting politicians and heads of state, et cetera.'

All this had been relayed to Suzy in a grim whisper, but now suddenly Jeff exclaimed excitedly, 'Look at that! Get that picture and I won't ever need to work again. Yes, you stay right there, baby,' he crooned to himself, before commanding Suzy, 'Come on! You'll have to distract the Colonel so that I can get this shot.'

'What? What am I supposed to do?' Suzy asked anxiously, and she looked to where the Colonel was standing casually in front of the two men, screening them from interruption.

Jeff gave her an exasperated look. 'Why the hell did they land me with you instead of someone who knows the ropes? I've heard that Roy has only taken you on as a favour, and because he likes your legs—he probably interviewed you imagining what they'd look like wrapped around him.'

Suzy struggled not to let Jeff see how upset she was by his comments. Her boss's openly sexual and often crude remarks to her were just one of the reasons why she was becoming increasingly unhappy about her job.

'You're a woman, aren't you? Go over there and do what comes naturally!' Jeff grunted, before pushing his way through the crowd, leaving Suzy to follow him.

Do what comes naturally! Oh, yes, she could quite easily do what came naturally with Colonel Soames… A thrill of dangerous emotion spiked through Suzy as she looked into the face of the man who was now standing right in front of her. He was, Suzy acknowledged, quite definitely the sexiest man she had ever seen. Those broad shoulders, that handsome face!

She was beginning to feel seriously alarmed by her reactions to him! Her friend Kate was always scolding her, telling her she didn't get out enough, and now Suzy thought she might be right. To be affected like this, to react like this simply at the sight of one specific man… She closed her eyes, willing herself to be sensible, and then opened them again.

What was it about a man in a dinner suit? What was it about *this* man in a dinner suit? Well, for one thing he was wearing his with an unselfconscious ease that said he was used to doing so, and for another it fitted him somehow as though it were a part of him. What had he looked like in his dress uniform? In combats? A tiny shudder ripped through her.

And as for that tan and those teeth…teeth that she was sure gleamed nearly as white as his shirtfront! And she was sure there were real muscles beneath all that tailoring as well.

Out of the corner of her eye she saw Jeff glowering at her. A little uncomfortably Suzy took a deep breath and stepped forward, a muddled plan of action forming inside her head. A smile of recognition at the Colonel then a brief apology for having mistaken him for someone else. A few seconds' work, but long enough, she hoped, for Jeff to get his picture.

Gritting her teeth against the knowledge that this kind of behaviour was quite definitely not her style, Suzy ignored the nervous churning of her stomach and stepped forward.

And then stopped! One step was all she had taken—so how come she now had her nose virtually against the Colonel's pristine white shirt? How had he moved without her being aware that he was doing so? When had he moved? Suzy wondered frantically. In less than a blink of the eye he had somehow gone from standing a couple of yards away to being right in front of her.

Suzy's sensitive nostrils started to quiver as she breathed in a discreet hint of cologne, underwritten by something very male and subtle that sent her self-control crashing into chaos.

He reached out and took hold of her arm, his grip firm and compelling. Suzy could feel her blood beating up around his encircling fingers as her body reacted to his hold.

Like someone lost in a trance she looked up at him. An instinct deeper than any thought or action seemed to have taken control of her, and she was powerless to do anything other than give in to it. The navy blue gaze fastened on her own. Her heart jerked against the wall of her chest, and the polite social apology she had been about to make died unspoken on her lips.

In a haze of dizzying desire Suzy felt her gaze slide like melting ice cream from the heat of his eyes to the curve of his mouth. Her whole body was galvanised by a series of tiny tremors and she exhaled on a small, soft, female sigh of wanton pleasure.

Without knowing what she was doing she lifted her free hand to trace the hard, firm line of his mouth—to see if the flesh there felt as erotic as it looked. But then her hand dropped to her side as another even more pleasurable way of conducting her survey struck her.

She had to reach up on her tiptoes in order to press her mouth to his, but the hand holding her arm seemed somehow to aid and balance her. The busy hum of conversation in the room faded as her lips made the discovery that just touching his mouth with her own was opening a door for her into a whole new world.

Blind and deaf to everything and everyone else around her, Suzy made a soft sound of pleasure deep in her throat. An aching whisper of female recognition.

Closing her eyes, she leaned into the male body, waiting hungrily for the Colonel to return the pressure of her lips, to part them with the swift, hard thrust of his tongue, to share with her the devouring intensity of need and longing that surged through her.

As she sighed her pleasure and hunger against his mouth she felt its pressure, his kiss heart-joltingly male. One of his hands slid firmly into the thick softness of her red-gold curls whilst the other pressed into the small of her back, urging her body closer to his own!

Suzy knew she was not very sexually experienced, and what was happening to her now was way out of her league! The way his mouth was moving on hers—firm, warm, knowing—the way his tongue-tip was laving the eager softness of her lips, was rewriting the logbook of her sexual history and adding a whole new chapter to it!

Lost in the rapture of what was happening to her, Suzy pressed closer, caught up in a cloud of hormone-drenched fantasy.

This was it! This was him! Her dragon-slayer and protector, the magical lover she had dreamed of in her most vulnerable moments. The hero she had secretly longed for all her life in her most private dreams. Her soul mate.

Suzy ached to tell him how she felt, how filled with delirious joy she was that he was here, how…

She gave a small shocked gasp as suddenly she was being pushed away.

Confusion darkened her eyes as she looked up at him, at a loss to understand what was happening until she saw the way he was looking back at her.

Instantly her joy was replaced with pain and despair. Shock gripped hold of her with icy fingers as she recognised the anger and loathing in the navy blue gaze boring into her.

'No!' She heard herself whisper the agonised denial, but it was no use. There was no mercy or softening in the hard, contemptuous gaze. Her whole body felt as though it was being drenched in shame and humiliation. Her soul mate? He was looking at her as though she were his worst enemy!

Anger, contempt, hostility, Suzy could see them all glittering in his eyes, before they were hidden away from her with a blank look of steely professionalism.

What on earth had she done? Why had she done it? She had made a complete and total fool of herself! What stupidity had made her resurrect that idiotic old dream of a soul mate? She'd thought she had had the sense to recognise it had no place in reality! It was a dream she had clung to for far too long anyway, like a child reluctant to relinquish the security of a worn-out teddy bear.

Her face was burning painfully—and not just because of the way he had looked at her. The shaky, sickly feeling invading her was surely a form of shock, a physical reaction to an emotional trauma. And she *was* traumatised, she admitted unwillingly. And not just by the Colonel's contempt and dislike!

Her own feelings had left her even more shocked and distressed...

She could feel his concentration on her, but she refused to look back at him. Because she was afraid to? Somewhere inside her head she could still feel the unspoken words 'I love you' banging frantically against the walls of their cage, like a tiny wounded bird desperate to escape. But Suzy knew they could never be set free. They had to be kept imprisoned for ever now, to protect her own sanity and self-respect!

'"*Down and Dirty* magazine."' She could hear him reading the name-badge she was wearing. 'I should have guessed. Your tactics are as cheap and tasteless as your articles.'

Savage pain followed by equally savage anger spiked into her heart. Illogically she felt as though somehow he had actively betrayed her by not recognising the person she really was, by misjudging her, not caring enough to recognise what had happened to her.

'I think your friend is waiting for you.'

The curt words were distinctly unfriendly, his voice clipped and incisive, and the look he gave her was coldly dismissive. But deep inside her Suzy could still feel the hard pressure of his mouth on hers.

Shaking, she turned to make her way towards the door, where Jeff was standing, an impassive bouncer holding his arm—and his camera.

Jeff's face, she saw with a sinking heart, was puce with temper.

'What the hell do you think you were doing?' he demanded once Suzy reached him. 'I told you to distract the guy, not eat him!'

Red-faced, Suzy couldn't think of anything to say to defend herself. 'Did you get your picture?'

'Yes! But if you hadn't been so busy playing kissy-face with the enemy you would have noticed that one of his gorillas was taking my camera off me! Good, was he? Yeah, I'll bet he was—after all, he's had plenty of experience. Like I said, during his last campaign a certain news reporter really had the hots for him. He's got quite a reputation with the female sex, has the Colonel. A killer instinct in bed and out of it.'

Suzy was beginning to feel nauseated, disgusted by what she was hearing. And even more so by her own idiotic gullibility. She couldn't understand her reaction—never mind her behaviour. She must be going crazy—and certainly her friend Kate would think so, if Suzy was ever foolish enough to tell her what had happened.

Kate and Suzy had been at university together, and Kate had kept in touch with Suzy when she had decided to drop out of her course and go home to nurse her mother through her final illness. Kate was married now, and with her husband ran a very successful small, independent travel agency.

Kate was constantly urging Suzy to enjoy life a little more, but Suzy still had debts to pay off—her student loan, for one thing, and the rent on the small flat she had shared with her widowed mother for another!

Thinking of her mother made Suzy's greeny-gold eyes darken. Her mother had been widowed before Suzy's birth, her father having been killed in a mountain-climbing accident. It was Suzy's belief that her mother had never got over the death of the man she loved, nor ceased blaming him for having died.

As she'd grown up Suzy had been the one who cared for her mother, rather than the other way around. Money had been tight, and Suzy had worked since her teens to help— first with a paper round and then at whatever unskilled work she could find.

Suzy remembered now that Kate often said she had an overdeveloped sense of responsibility and that she allowed others to put upon her. She couldn't imagine Colonel Lucas James Soames ever allowing anyone to put upon him, Suzy decided bitterly. If anyone were foolish enough to turn to him for help or compassion he would immediately reject them!

Suzy tensed, angry with herself for allowing the Colonel into her thoughts. And yet running beneath her anger, like a silent and dangerously racing river, she could still feel an unwanted ache of pain. Fear curled through her with soft, deadly tendrils. Why had she had such an extraordinary reaction to him? She wasn't that sort of person. Those emotions, that fierce rush of sexual longing, just weren't her! She gave a small shudder of distaste.

It was an experience she was better off forgetting—pretending had never happened, in fact!

And that was exactly what she intended to do!

Luke studied the schedules in front of him. Meticulously detailed plans for his upcoming work. The Prince had hinted that he would like him on board for his permanent staff, but that kind of role wasn't one Luke wanted. Perhaps his American mother's blood was responsible for that! He had never been someone who enjoyed mundane routine. Even as a boy he had liked the challenge of pushing back boundaries and continually learning and growing.

His parents had died in an accident when he was eleven years old. The Army had sent him home to his grandmother and the comfortable country house where his father had grown up. His grandmother had done her best, but Luke had felt constricted at the boarding school she had sent him to. Even then he had known he would follow his father into the Army, and the happiest day of his life had been the day he had finally been free to follow that ambition.

The Army had been not just his career but his family as well. Until recently. Until he had woken up one morning and realised that he had had enough of witnessing other people's pain and death. That his ears had grown too sensitive to the screams of wounded children and his eyes too hurt by the sight of thin and starving bodies. He had seen it happen too many times before to other soldiers to hesitate. His emotions were getting in the way of his professionalism. It was time for him to move on!

The Army had tried to persuade him to change his mind. There had been talk of further promotion. But Luke had refused to be swayed. In his own mind he was no longer a totally effective soldier. Given the choice between destroying an enemy and protecting a child Luke knew he could no longer guarantee he would put the former first.

And working for His Royal Highness was definitely not for him! Too tame after the demands of Army life. Although there were some similarities between the two! He started to frown. Female reporters! He loathed and despised them! They were a hundred times worse than their male equivalent, in Luke's opinion. He had seen at first hand the damage they could wreak in their determination to get a story. A shadow of pain momentarily darkened his eyes, and the newly healed wound just below his hipbone seemed to pulse.

And as for the lengths such women were prepared to go!

His mouth hardened. So far as he was concerned Suzy Roberts and her ilk were as contemptible as the rags they worked for.

Reporter? Scavenger was a more appropriate word.

He turned his attention back to his paperwork, but, maddeningly, she would not be ejected from his thoughts.

What the hell was the matter with him that he should be wasting his time thinking about Suzy Roberts? That auburn hair and the way her gold-green gaze fastened on him must have addled his brain.

Had she really thought he was so idiotic that he would be deceived by that obviously fake look of longing she had given him? That equally fake tremor he had felt run right through her body when he had touched her? And as for that faint but unmistakable scent he could have sworn he could still smell...

Angrily he got up and strode across the room, pushing open a window, letting in an icy cold blast of air. Perhaps the unintentional celibacy of his life over these last few years had suddenly begun to affect him. But to such an extent that he wanted a woman like Suzy Roberts?

Like hell he did! But the sudden tension in his groin told a different story.

It was late, and he had a business appointment to keep. Finishing what he was doing, he made his way from the office to the privacy of his own apartment, automatically watching and checking as he did so. Once a commando always a commando—even when he could no longer...

Suppressing thoughts he did not want to have to deal with, Luke walked into his suite and headed for the shower.

Stripping off, he stepped into it, the hot needle-jets of water glistening on his body as he moved beneath the shower's spray. The light fell on old scars on his chest, and the newer one low down on his body.

Having finished showering, he stepped out onto the marble floor, padding naked into his bedroom to extract a pair of clean white boxer shorts from a drawer. The phrase 'going commando-style' might have a certain sexual edge to it when used to describe the choice not to wear any underwear, but from his own point of view weeks, sometimes months of living in the field, in one set of sweat and dirt-soaked combats had given him a very different take on the matter! To anyone who had experienced desert combat conditions the luxury of quantities of clean water was something to be truly appreciated.

CHAPTER TWO

Six months later

SUZY paused and studied the sleek yachts clustered in the harbour of the small Italian coastal resort. Two women walked past her, expensively groomed and wearing equally expensive designer clothes. Suzy had dressed as appropriately as she could for this luxurious resort, in white linen trousers and a brief sleeveless matching top, with sandals on her feet and the *de rigueur* sunglasses concealing her eyes, but no way was she in their league—and no way was she made for such an exclusive resort.

She had tried to tell Kate as much when her friend had announced that since she and her husband could not take up the week's holiday they had been offered via their business they wanted to give the treat to Suzy instead.

30

'Oh, no, Kate, I couldn't possibly accept your generosity,' Suzy had protested.

'It isn't generosity,' Kate had retorted. 'You need this break, Suzy. You've been through a lot these last few years—nursing your mother and then losing her, working every spare hour you had to finish your degree, and then that awful job you had!'

Suzy had sighed. 'I shouldn't have handed in my notice, really. My tutor had been so kind, getting the intro for me, I feel so guilty.'

'You feel guilty?' Kate had exploded. 'Why on earth should you? You said yourself that you hated the way the magazine worked, its lack of morality with regard to how it got its stories and everything. And when I think of the way that slimy boss of yours tried to behave towards you! If anyone should be feeling guilty it's them, not you, Suzy! I'm surprised they're allowed to get away with treating you as they did. You know my opinion—you should have reported them for sexual harassment!'

Just listening to Kate's words had been enough to make Suzy shudder a little.

'It wasn't as easy as that, Kate,' Suzy had reminded her. 'For one thing I was the only female working there. No one would have backed me up.'

Hearing the strain in her friend's voice, Kate had shot her a quick look of concern before continuing, 'Suzy, I know how strong you are, and how independent, but please just for once put yourself first. You need this break. You need time to relax and reflect, to pick up the threads of your life and weave them into a new pattern. You need this breathing space! I want to do this for you and I shall be very hurt if you refuse.'

Put like that, how could she refuse? Suzy had acknowledged ruefully. And besides, there had been enough truth in what Kate had said to make her see that her friend was right.

She still shook with anxiety and nervous tension when she thought about the scene in the *Down and Dirty* office the day she had handed in her notice. The crude insults her boss had hurled at her still made her face burn with embarrassment and loathing.

'You aren't leaving—I'm sacking you,' he had told her furiously. 'No jumped-up little nothing is going to mess me about!'

He had then claimed publicly that he was sacking her because she had offered him sex in exchange for promotion—but privately told her he would rescind his claim if she agreed to go to bed with him.

Her flesh still crawled at the thought.

Roy Jarvis might be the magazine's editor-in-chief, but so far as Suzy was concerned he was the most morally corrupt man she had ever met. And her opinion was not just based on his attitude towards her, but on the way he ran the magazine and obtained its articles. Roy Jarvis's reporters were told to let nothing stop them in their pursuit of obtaining a story. She had been like a fish out of water in such an environment.

And Kate had been right, Suzy acknowledged unhappily now. She *did* need some time out to reassess her life. And her emotions.

Suzy closed her eyes and tried to swallow past the hard ball of pain and misery lodged in her throat. Panic prickled over her skin as she fought against allowing herself to think about the cause of her pain.

Instead she switched her mind to more easily dealt with issues. The difficulties of the past few years, then the misery of realising she was in a job she hated, and working with people whose morals she could never accept, never mind adopt, had all affected her. But she still needed to earn a living—somehow! And giving in to Kate and accepting this holiday was not, in her opinion, going to aid that.

No, but it might stop her from dreaming about a man she should have forgotten.

And this pretty Italian fishing village, perched precariously on the steep sides of a small bay, was surely a perfect spot in which to chill out and ground herself, to assess her own ambitions and think again about her original desire to become an archivist, perhaps. Her tutor had scorned her ambition, but Suzy had a deep longing for the cloistered quiet of such career.

Skirting the pretty harbour, with its chic and very expensive restaurants, Suzy headed for the steep path that led to the top of the cliff.

Half an hour later she had reached it, and she paused to study the magnificent view and to take a couple of photographs to show Kate.

Another hill rose up a short way along the path, and Suzy headed for it, wondering what lay beyond.

Its incline was steep, and she was a little out of breath when she finally made it to the top. She gasped, her eyes widening in delight as she looked down into the lush valley below her at the stunningly beautiful Palladan villa at its centre. She just had to get a photo of it to show Kate and her husband.

Rummaging in her bag, she found the small digital camera Kate had insisted on lending her.

'If you get any really good pictures we can put them on our Web site,' she had announced when Suzy had tried to protest.

The camera was obviously expensive, and Suzy had said as much, but Kate had dismissed her concern, shrugging it aside as she reassured her, 'It's insured—and if you do lose it—which I know you won't—then we shall replace it.'

Dutifully Suzy had photographed everything she thought might be of interest to her friend, and she knew that Kate would love this wonderful villa in its beautiful setting. From her vantage point Suzy could see the layout of its formal gardens within the high walls surrounding them, and the lake that lay beyond with its picturesque grotto.

Carefully she focused on the villa, pausing for a moment, as sunlight glinted on the metal casing, to stare in bemused awe at the sight of four imposingly large men in military uniform heading for an even equally imposing large black Mercedes, almost hidden from view beyond the entrance to the villa.

What an impressive sight! She had to get a photograph of it—and of them! Who on earth were they?

On his way across the courtyard—having escorted the private security officers who had arrived to check out the villa without giving any warning, and against Luke's strict instructions, to their huge Mercedes with its blacked-out windows—Luke froze as he caught the unmistakable glint of sunlight on metal. Automatically he reached for his binoculars, training the powerful lens on the steep hillside above the villa.

He had done everything he could to avoid having to take on this commission, but pressure had been put on him, via his old commanding officer and certain other people, and reluctantly he had given in—although not without first enquiring grimly why on earth MI5 operatives could not be used.

'Because it is so sensitive, old boy,' had been the wry answer he had received. 'And because we don't have anyone in the field of your calibre.'

Reluctantly Luke had bowed to the pressure he'd been under.

Making sure that the Foreign Secretary was able to conduct a very politically sensitive meeting with the President of a certain turbulent African state, without either arousing the curiosity of the press or certain factions within the African state required optimum vigilance. And why on earth anyone had ever thought it a good idea to conduct such an exercise so close to a popular Italian resort—visited by the rich and famous and followed there by the paparazzi—Luke had no way of knowing.

Of course he had tried to initiate a change of venue, but he had been overruled.

A smooth-talking suit from MI5 had announced that no one would suspect that the Foreign Secretary would be seeing anyone political whilst enjoying a holiday with his children.

Children? Luke had baulked furiously at that point. No matter how many reassurances or platitudes the MI5 suit might choose to utter, this was potentially a dangerous mission.

The African President was insisting on bringing his own private guards with him, and he was a man who was obsessed with a fear of betrayal—both at home and abroad. If things should go pear-shaped Luke did not want to have to worry about two young children as well as their father. He had said as much to Sir Peter Verey when they had been introduced, suggesting that his children might be better left with their mother.

'My dear chap,' had been Sir Peter's drawled response. 'I wish I could oblige, but you see my ex-wife is insistent that they come with me. Thinks I'm not doing my fatherly duty and that sort of thing.'

Luke knew all about Sir Peter Verey's ex-wife. She had left him for a billionaire industrialist who had little liking of his predecessor's offspring, with the result that she had placed both children at boarding school.

Luke frowned as he swept the hillside for whoever had been responsible for that telltale glint.

The resort less than a couple of miles away seethed with celebrities and minor continental royals, all of whom seemed to be followed by their own pack of predators, feeding off them as if they were carrion.

It didn't take Luke's trained eye long to find its quarry—in fact, he reflected in disgust, it did not need a trained eye to spot her at all. She was standing there openly photographing the villa. She? Luke frowned as he studied the familiar features. Suzy Roberts! It was as little effort for him to conjure up her name as it had been for him to recognise her face. Suzy Roberts, reporter for *Down and Dirty* magazine. Automatically he swept the area around her to see if she was on her own, before focusing on her once again.

She looked thinner, paler—and what the hell was she doing standing in the strong sunlight without the protection of a hat when any fool could see that she had the kind of delicate skin that would burn?

How on earth had she got wind of what was going on? The editor of the magazine she worked for got his stories by trawling in the gutter for them.

Luke's mouth compressed. The gutter, maybe, but then Roy Jarvis did specialise in 'revealing' the failings and vices of those in power, as well as breaking some extraordinarily sensitive news stories. Someone was supplying him with his information, and Luke knew that if he had been in charge of finding out who it was the leak would have been stopped a long time ago.

Luke refused to believe that anyone could have got through his own rigorous security, but he was not the only person who knew what was happening. Somehow Roy Jarvis had been given a tip-off about the upcoming meeting, and he had obviously sent Suzy Roberts to find out what she could and confirm the story so that he could publish it.

After all, a reporter like Suzy had the extra assistance of her sexuality to help her get her story—and she would have no qualms about using it!

Lucas had seen it happen over and over again in the theatre of war, and of course he had already discovered for himself that there were no lengths Suzy Roberts was not prepared to go!

Silently Luke slipped out of the villa grounds, moving quickly and stealthily towards his quarry.

Oblivious to the danger, Suzy pushed her hair back off her face. The villa really was a gem. She paused to admire it again before lifting the camera to take another shot.

Luke, who had circled up behind her, waited until she had raised the camera before making his move.

As Suzy focused the camera he reached for it...

Someone was trying to steal the camera!

Instinctively Suzy turned round, and then froze in shocked disbelief whilst Luke took it from her.

'What are you doing?' she demanded as soon as she could speak.

Lucas Soames—here! She could feel the colour leaving her face and then surging back into it. Her heart was thudding in panic, and she felt as though she was trembling from head to foot. Emotions she had assured herself she had totally destroyed were taking a frightening hold on her, threatening to swamp her.

Frantically she tried to ignore them, to focus instead on what she should be feeling. These emotions had no right to exist. Lucas Soames meant nothing to her, and one of the reasons she was here on holiday was to make sure she was fully recovered from whatever it was she had experienced six months ago.

Willing her physical reaction to him to subside, Suzy demanded sharply, 'Give me back my camera!'

Her eyes widened as she watched Lucas delete the pictures she had just taken.

'No!' she protested, trying to snatch back the camera, to stop him ruining her photographs.

Luke reacted immediately, fending her off with one deceptively easy movement that kept her at arm's length from him, his fingers locked around her wrist as he finished what he was doing.

Despairingly Suzy closed her eyes, trying to blot out the physical reality of him in an effort to protect herself. But almost immediately she realised her mistake. Deprived of sight, she felt all her sensory receptors focusing instead on the feel of Lucas Soames's hand around her wrist—the texture of his flesh, the powerful strength of his grip, the coolness of his skin against the heat of her own. Weakening thrills of sensation were running up her arm, and she could feel the frantic jump of her pulse.

Panic and desperation speared through her. 'What are you doing?' she demanded, the sound of her voice raw and frantic in her ears as she recognised her fear and the reason for it.

What was it about this man that made her feel like this?

Luke studied her silently, assessing her behaviour and her reactions. She looked convincingly both distraught and distressed, and he mentally applauded her acting talent whilst cynically wondering how many victims she had honed it on.

Ignoring her anxious question, he asked one of his own. 'Why were you photographing the villa?'

His response caught Suzy off guard.

There was something about the coldly intense way he was watching her that unnerved her, and Suzy felt a shudder of apprehension run through her body. Stubbornly she fought against giving in to it—and to him!

'Why shouldn't I?' she shot back. Antagonism towards him was a far safer emotion than that dangerous and overwhelming surge of longing she had experienced the last time she had seen him. Don't think about it, she warned herself frantically. Don't remember. Don't feel...

Seeing him then had been like having the clouds part to reveal a miraculous space of blue sky and a dizzying vision of heaven. But things were different now, she reassured herself fiercely. *She* was different now!

Taking a deep breath, Suzy gave a deliberately nonchalant shrug before saying, 'That's what people on holiday do—take photographs.'

Her body language was flawless, Luke acknowledged grudgingly. Not by so much as the flicker of one of those ridiculously long eyelashes of hers was she revealing the fact that she was lying. He could feel his temper starting to rise. Immediately he checked it, alarmed that somehow she had managed to pierce the shield of his professionalism.

'On holiday?' He gave Suzy a comprehensive and cynical look. 'Oh, come on—you can come up with something better than that, surely?'

Just looking at her now—anger sparking her eyes to brilliant gold, flushing her cheeks with heat—anyone other than him would have believed immediately that she was a woman righteously defending herself from an unwarranted attack. But he knew she had to be lying, given who she was, and sure enough, as he continued to watch her, she was unable to continue to return his gaze.

What was Lucas Soames trying to say? Suzy wondered frantically. Had he guessed how he had affected her? Did he think she was nursing some kind of desire for him and that she had followed him here?

Her face began to burn again. If he did then she was going to make sure...

'Nice camera.' Luke interrupted her thoughts, adding assessingly, 'Expensive too.' Still nervously on edge, Suzy told him stiffly, 'It isn't mine...it belongs to a friend.'

Luke could see the discomfort and the guilt in her eyes—but, to his own irritated disbelief, the knowledge that he was right to be suspicious of her made him feel more angry than satisfied. Determined to stamp on such feelings and destroy them, he responded coldly, 'A friend? So, Roy Jarvis is a friend now, is he, as well as your employer?'

Her employer!

Suzy shook her head.

'I don't work for the magazine any more,' she told him quickly. 'I…I left.' Even saying the words was enough to bring back the unpleasant memories, and she had to swallow against the bile of her distress.

'Oh, come on. You don't really expect me to fall for that, do you?' Luke demanded unpleasantly.

'It's true,' Suzy insisted fiercely. 'I no longer work for the magazine. You can check if you don't believe me!'

Her eyes were more green than gold now, Luke recognised. Reflecting her passionate nature? He frowned, irritated with himself for allowing his attention to be distracted from the professional to the personal.

'Oh, I have no doubt that officially you might have left, but it isn't unheard of for your boss, your *friend,* to use underhand methods to get what he wants. He has sent you here to work undercover—which is, as we both know, why you are up here photographing the villa and spying!'

Now cynicism had joined the cold disdain icing his voice, and Suzy decided that she had had enough. Not allowing him to finish, she interrupted him hotly.

'That's ridiculous! Why on earth would he send me to do that? It's the resort that is full of the glitterati, not this villa, and as for my agreeing to spy on anyone—I have my own moral code!' She gave him a bitingly scornful look, but her glare might have been directed at an invisible shield for all the effect it had on its intended victim.

'Very affecting.' Luke stopped her. 'But you are wasting your breath and my time with this unconvincing show of innocence. I know exactly what you are, remember? I've witnessed your professional reporting methods—and your *moral code*—at first hand,' he reminded her grimly.

A telltale crimson tide of guilt and misery flooded Suzy's face. Illogically she felt not just humiliated by his words but emotionally hurt as well.

How could he say something like that to her? Hadn't he been able to tell that she had kissed him because of her own overwhelming need to do so and not for any other reason?

Unable to stop herself, Suzy discovered that she was reliving the feelings she had had then. Anguish filled her. Did he really think she was the kind of woman who would do such a thing for any other reason than because she simply had not been able to stop herself?

The very thought of what he had implied disgusted and nauseated her, and she burst out defensively, 'That wasn't—I didn't—I did it because—'

Abruptly Luke stopped her again. 'You did it because you thought it would be an excellent way of providing a firescreen for your companion—yes, I know that!' he told her grimly. 'Unfortunately for you it wasn't very effective.' He paused, and then added curtly, 'And neither was the kiss!'

What the hell was he thinking of? Luke asked himself savagely as his comment fell into the silence between them and he was forced to remember the kiss they had shared. A woman as experienced as this one must have felt his body's arousal, and gloated over his response to her. Any minute now she would be reminding him of it and challenging him to deny it. And there was no way Luke wanted to be dragged into that dangerous and unreliable ground.

Yes, he had responded to her. He could not deny that! Yes, he had for a split second in time experienced the most extraordinary physical longing for her, and the most extraordinary emotions. But that had been a momentary weakness, quickly controlled, and of no lasting or real importance whatsoever!

'What did Jarvis tell you to do—apart from take photographs?' he demanded sharply, steering his questions back in the right direction.

Still grappling with her own feelings, Suzy told him angrily, 'He didn't tell me to do anything!'

Her anger must somehow have heightened her senses, she decided, because suddenly she was aware of the musky male scent of Lucas Soames's body. She could see the sunlight glinting on the fine dark hair of his muscular forearms. Her heart somersaulted and then attempted a cartwheel, crashing into her chest wall as it did so. She willed herself to drag her gaze away from his body, but somehow it was impossible to do so. The white tee shirt he was wearing, although not tight-fitting, still revealed an impressive breadth of shoulder and chest. Something dangerous was happening to her, and she seemed powerless to stop it.

Suzy began to panic.

The back of her head was burning from the heat of the sun. It was making her feel slightly sick and dizzy—or was it the intensity of the navy blue gaze, the shock of her own emotions that was responsible for her malaise?

She couldn't give in to such feelings, Suzy warned herself frantically. She must not give in to them! She must think of something else! She must get away from here—get away from here and from Lucas Soames, and the sooner the better. If she didn't leave, if she was forced to stay, she was terrified that she might be trapped into saying something that would betray how she felt about him. How she *had* felt about him, she corrected herself. Taking a deep breath, she searched for the right words.

'I'm sorry if you feel you can't believe me,' she began politely. 'But I assure you that I am telling you the truth. I do not work for the magazine any more and no one from it is responsible for my being here! Like I just told you, I am here on holiday!'

She was picking her words too carefully for them to be genuine, Luke decided.

'On holiday? Alone?' he challenged her softly. One dark eyebrow rose tellingly, and

Suzy was hotly conscious of his merciless and unkind gaze sweeping her face and then her body.

'I needed time on my own…to…to think…'

She had to get away from him!

'Time on your own? A woman like you?'

The razor-edge contempt in his voice made her face burn, but before she could say anything he continued silkily, 'So, if you aren't, as you claim, working for Roy Jarvis any more, then who are you working for?'

His question caught Suzy off guard, and she had to wrench her thoughts away from the pain his insult had caused her in order to answer it.

'I'm not working for anyone at the moment. I haven't got another job yet…at least…' She paused, her eyes darkening as his question reactivated her own anxiety about her future. After the contempt he had already shown her there was no way she was going to tell him that in order to make ends meet she had taken a job in a local super-market.

Suddenly she had had enough.

'Why are you questioning me like this?' she demanded wearily. 'Just because you're here, guarding some government bigwig, that doesn't give you the right to...to treat me as some kind of...of criminal. What is it? Why are you looking at me like that?' she demanded nervously, fear trickling through her veins as she sensed that somehow something had changed, that the anger she had sensed in him before had been replaced by a steely determination.

'How do you know who is staying at the villa?' Luke questioned quietly.

For a moment Suzy was too bemused to answer him. Was it *that* that was responsible for the intimidating change in him?

'I heard someone talking about it,' she told him honestly. 'I thought he was supposed to be here on holiday, but of course now that I've seen you, and those men who were leaving, I realise...'

Her voice trailed away, when she saw his expression, and Luke prompted her softly.

'Yes? What is it exactly that you now realise? Something you know your boss Jarvis would be very interested in? Something that you just can't wait to report to him?'

Suzy stared at him aghast.

'No! No—nothing like that. He isn't my boss anymore,' she denied. 'I've already told you that.'

Something about the way he was watching her made her feel very afraid.

'So I was right.'

Suzy could feel her heart bumping heavily against her ribs as the deceptively soft words penetrated her awareness.

'You realise, of course, what this means?'

Suzy stared at him uncomprehendingly. He had lost her completely now, she acknowledged, and she fought to drag her unwilling mind away from her worry about the physical effect Lucas Soames was having on her emotions to what he was saying to her.

'What *what* means?' she asked.

Lucas's mouth thinned. He had no time for games, no matter how much Suzy Roberts might enjoy her play-acting. One minute the *ingénue*, another the *femme fatale*. A tiny muscle twitched in his jaw as he tensed his body against memories he didn't want to have. Memories of the feel of Suzy's body against his own, the taste of her mouth, the scent of her skin…

Savagely he turned away from her. This— she—was a complication he just did not need. It was bad enough that Jarvis had sent anyone here at all—but that it should be her!

Angrily, he examined the facts—and his options! Yes, they both knew why Suzy was here, but just how much did she know? How much information did she actually have?

He had destroyed the photographs she had taken of the African President's private guards, but he could not eradicate that information from her memory. And he certainly could not allow her to pass it on to anyone else—and most especially not to Roy Jarvis, to publish in his wretched magazine!

There was only one thing he could do now, little as he relished the prospect!

Luke had had his fill of reporters, both male and female! He had seen at first hand the damage, the devastation their single-minded determination could cause. He had seen fighting men's lives risked and innocent civilians' lives lost for the sake of a 'hot' story. And he had seen... His mouth twisted, his expression hardening even further.

He'd seen children under school age, half starved, fighting for water and food...whilst excited reporters tried to film their pitiable situation. And worse! Much, much worse! He moved, and the scar low on his belly pulled against the wound it covered.

He had learned over the years to mistrust the media at large.

And Ms Suzy Roberts was not going to be an exception to his rule that all media personnel were to be treated as guilty and kept under strict surveillance!

Luke's gaze narrowed.

Despite the fact that he was trained to keep his body still for hours on end, he suddenly felt he needed to move, step back a little from Suzy, and he grimly suppressed the unwanted knowledge that her proximity was affecting him.

'You realise, of course, that I can't let you tell anyone what you've seen?' Luke informed her.

A cold thrill of horror ran through her.

'But I'm not going to tell anyone,' she protested.

'I suppose the best and easiest thing to do would be for me to confiscate your passport and then have you thrown in jail,' Luke said calmly.

'What?' Suzy's face paled. 'No—you can't do that...' She could hardly believe what she was hearing, but one look at Lucas Soames's face assured her that he was deadly serious.

'Oh, I think you'll find that I can,' Luke assured her. 'But, knowing what you are capable of doing in order to get what you want, I think the best place for you right now is where I can make sure you aren't able to make any kind of contact with Roy Jarvis.'

'What—what are you going to do?' Suzy asked anxiously,

'I'm going to take you back to the villa with me—as my partner.'

CHAPTER THREE

'*WHAT?*'

Suzy was totally lost for words as she struggled to comprehend what he had said. His partner! But that meant... Fear and then longing shot through her like a firework showering her insides and touching every single nerve-ending she possessed. Partners... lovers...soul mates! No. She just wasn't strong enough to withstand this kind of torture!

'No—no! You can't do that. I won't!' she protested shakily.

He had already released her wrist, and as she spoke she was backing away from him, adrenalin pulsing through her veins. She had to get away! She had to!

As soon as she was out of his arm's reach she turned and started to run, driven by her instinct to flee, to protect herself, to hide herself from the danger she knew lay waiting for her!

Intent on her escape, she did not even think about sticking to the path which led back to the resort, instead plunging headlong straight down the steep hillside, sending up a shower of dry earth and small stones as she did so.

Luke watched her, knowing how easily he could catch her, his grim look turning to a frown as he saw the obstacle ahead of her— a large boulder, right in her path. He waited for her to change direction to avoid it, knowing that if she didn't—if she ran right into it—which she *was* going to do!

He caught her with a couple of yards to spare, knocking the breath out of her body as she fell towards the ground. But somehow, to Suzy's astonishment, before she hit the ground their positions were reversed, and it was Lucas Soames who was lying on the hard earth, with her held fast on top of him. His arms were fastened around her like iron bands, one gripping her body the other cradling her head.

Winded and frightened, Suzy tried to free herself—only to find that she could hardly move.

'Let go of me!' she demanded, struggling frantically.

'Stop that, you little fool, otherwise we'll both be—' Lucas began, and then stopped as one of Suzy's flailing hands caught the side of his mouth.

Against instinct, certainly against training, and surely against wanting, he opened his mouth and caught hold of the two offending fingers.

Heat and shock poured through Suzy's body.

Lucas Soames had her fingers in his mouth and he was...

She completely forgot what had been happening, and her own desperate attempt to break free of his imprisonment of her. Her body, her mind, her heart—all flooded with pure undistilled pleasure as his tongue slowly caressed her flesh.

The warm, wet slide of his tongue against her fingers caused images of shocking and unfamiliar sensuality to burst into her head. She wanted to replace her fingers with her mouth, her tongue. She wanted... Suzy could feel the dangerous familiarity of the ache inside her, in her breasts and low down in her body.

Desperate to protect herself, she wrenched her fingers away.

Deprived of the feel of her soft, sweet flesh against his tongue, Luke reacted immediately. The hand at the back of her head forced her towards him, and his mouth covered hers in devastatingly sensual punishment.

Suzy tried to resist but it was too late. Her lips were betraying her, softening beneath those of her captor!

And it was no wonder Lucas Soames was taking their reaction as an indication that she was inviting him to investigate their closed line, to torment it with the firm flick of his tongue. He probed the effectiveness of her defence and discovered that it was all too easily penetrated.

Held fast on top of him, his hands controlling her ability to move, there was nothing Suzy could do other than submit.

Submit? This was submission? This eager opening of her lips? This hungry greeting of his tongue with her own? This feeling that was spiking through her, impaling her on a rack of tormented feverish longing and need, whilst her hands gripped his shoulders and she forgot every single word of the promises she had made to herself. She was responding to him! Allowing herself to be deceived that the fierce, demanding pressure of his mouth on hers meant something! That the feeling possessing her was also possessing him. That they were...soul mates?

She gave a small gasp.

Luke wrenched his mouth from Suzy's, his fingers biting into her soft flesh as he tried to find a logical explanation for what he had done.

And for what he was feeling!

He could feel his muscles straining as he willed his aroused body into submission. What the hell was happening to him? Physically he might be able to contain what he was feeling—the urgency of his arousal, the savage need he had to hold her and possess her—but it was what was going on inside his head, not his body, that was causing him the most concern. He had never mixed his professional life and his private life. And he had certainly never needed anyone with the intensity with which he had just been driven to possess Suzy Roberts's mouth!

Angrily he fought to ignore both the ache the loss of contact with Suzy's body was causing him and the inner voice that was urging him to continue, to possess the soft warmth of her breasts with his hands, to stroke and explore their feminine softness until he could feel the tight buds of her nipples rising to his touch...

Furious with himself, Luke checked his erotic thoughts.

'Let go of you?' he challenged Suzy, as if the kiss had never happened, angling their bodies so that she could see the rocks below them. 'Take a look! You were heading right for them, and if I hadn't stopped you right now you would be down there.'

Lifting her head cautiously, Suzy looked down the hillside, her stomach lurching as the saw the jagged rock less than a yard away from them.

'I wasn't anywhere near it,' she lied.

But she was shuddering, and for some reason she was closing her eyes and turning her face into his shoulder.

Immediately Luke stopped her, his fingers digging into her arms as he held her away, a look of tightly reined anger compressing his mouth.

'If I'd any sense I should have let you go ahead,' she heard him muttering. 'It would have saved me a hell of a lot of trouble.'

He loathed and despised her that much?

'Then why didn't you? I can assure you that as far as I am concerned it would have

been preferable to what I've just been sub-
jected to!'

Luke had an almost violent need to take
her back in his arms and prove to her that she
was lying, but instead he derided, 'If that's
your way of trying to persuade me you're
someone who'd choose death before dishon-
our, you are wasting your time!'

It wasn't him who was causing her such
pain, it was her own anger, Suzy told herself
fiercely.

She couldn't bring herself to look down at
those rocks again, and she couldn't escape
from the knowledge that if he hadn't actually
saved her life then he had certainly saved her
from hurting herself very badly.

No, she couldn't escape from that knowledge, and it seemed that she couldn't escape
from him either. Right now, whilst the solid
protection of his hard body beneath her own
and the equally hard feel of his arms around
her body might be protecting her physically,
emotionally this kind of intimacy with him
was not doing her any favours at all.

Emotionally? What was she thinking? Suzy knew perfectly well what she was thinking, even if she did not want to acknowledge it. With just one searing kiss Lucas Soames had shown her that, far from being over what she had fought so hard to convince herself had been a moment of uncharacteristic silliness the first time she had seen him, she was if any thing even more vulnerable to him now.

But not for much longer, Suzy promised herself determinedly.

She made a small movement, impatient to be free of him, and then froze with disbelief at the speed with which her flesh reacted to her careless action.

Her face was burning with mortified embarrassment, and she prayed that Lucas Soames could not feel, as she could, the sudden sensual tensing and swelling of her breasts. Her nipples were tightening and thrusting against her top, as though eager for his attention, whilst her stomach clenched and a slow ache possessed the lower part of her body. The urge to put her hand over her sex to quell its silent demand was so strong that it was just as well that his hold of her prevented her from doing so.

Prevented her from doing that, yes, but it didn't prevent her from reacting to the intimate pressure of his body against hers, and the soft mound covering her sex began to swell wantonly, a totally unfamiliar desire to grind her hips against him pulsing through her with increasingly demanding intensity.

Engrossed in her own dismay, she heard Lucas saying harshly, 'Unfortunately for me, on this occasion at least, I prefer to protect human life rather than to destroy it.'

'Protect human life?' Suzy demanded scornfully, secretly relieved to be able to focus on something other than her unwanted reaction to him. 'You were a soldier! Soldiers don't protect lives,' she told him with hostility. 'They—'

She wasn't allowed to get any further. His hold on her tightened. She could see the anger darkening his eyes as he looked at her, and her heart jolted painfully against her ribs.

'I suppose I should have expected that kind of ill-informed and gratuitously offensive remark from someone like you,' he said with scathing contempt. 'In the modern Army our purpose is to do the job we have to do with as little loss of human life as possible!'

His reaction had been immediate and savage—and surely out of proportion to what she had said, Suzy reflected inwardly, refusing to allow herself to be intimidated by it. He might generally prefer to save lives, but in her case she suspected he would have been more than ready to make an exception, if instinct and training had not been so ingrained in him!

Women reporters! Lucas felt the sour taste of old bitterness clogging his throat. And yet despite everything he was still holding on to her. He was holding on to her because he wasn't going to risk so much as letting her move a foot from his side, Luke assured himself acidly.

Even so...

'Time to go,' he announced, moving so swiftly that Suzy could barely catch her breath.

One moment she was lying on top of him on the ground, the next somehow she was standing up on her own, with Lucas next to her.

'Go?' she questioned warily 'You're going to let me go?'

That surely wasn't disappointment that was dampening down her relief, was it?

'I give you my word that I won't say anything about the villa to anyone,' she began to assure him earnestly.

'Your word?' Lucas rapped out contemptuously. 'We both know that your word is as worthless and overused—as...as you are yourself!'

The pain was everywhere. Inside her head, inside her heart, inside her body. With every breath she took she was breathing in its poison, its rank bitterness contaminating her.

Worthless...overused... Immediately Suzy wanted to hit back at him, to hurt him as deeply as he had hurt her, to mark him in a way that would leave him wounded for life, as she knew she herself would be.

Some women might shrug it off and even laugh at such a branding, but she was not one of them.

Overused. That was what he thought of her. She felt sick inside with emotional agony.

Something had changed. Some subtle shifting had occurred that had wrongfooted him, Luke's instincts told him. But he couldn't fathom what it was.

Suzy was staring fixedly past him, her body immobile. Was it her silence that was triggering the sixth sense that told him he had overlooked something? Had he expected her to argue with him, try to win him round, convince him that he was wrong and that she was to be trusted?

Frowning, he looked away, and so didn't see the single tear that welled in each of

Suzy's eyes, to hang glistening on her eyelashes before rolling down her face.

His words had hurt more than if he had physically attacked her—more than if he had turned and walked away from her—more than if he had simply left her to die in a crushed heap of flesh and bones against the jagged rocks from which he had saved her. One day she would be grateful for them, she promised herself. One day she would look back on this and know that what he had said to her had destroyed every minute seed of feeling she might have had for him with the force of a nuclear attack.

One day. But not this day. This day she felt as though she wanted to crawl into a hole and hide herself away, somewhere private and dark, where she and the pain would be alone to confront one another.

CHAPTER FOUR

SUZY could feel her legs trembling as she took a step away from Lucas Soames, her gaze fixed on the path ahead.

Did she really think he was just going to let her walk away? Luke could not credit her woeful lack of reality. He had grabbed her before she had taken more than a few paces, jerking her back towards him.

Suzy only had time to recognise that despite his violent gesture he did not actually hurt her before she was clamped to his side.

'You'd better get one thing clear,' Luke told her curtly. 'From now on where I go, you go. And you can take your choice whether it is by my side, two steps ahead of me or two steps behind. But two steps is going to be as far away as I let you get.'

'You can't do that. You can't make me!' Suzy protested shakily, real fear in her eyes as she looked at him.

'I can and will do anything and everything I deem necessary in order to protect the interests I am here to protect,' Lucas told her uncompromisingly. 'Now,' he demanded, 'where are you staying?'

Mutinously Suzy refused to answer him, compressing her lips and looking away from him. Out of the corner of her eye she saw him shrug.

'Very well then, we'll go straight to the villa. If you choose to spend the next few weeks with only the clothes you are now wearing, then you may do so!'

Unable to stop herself, Suzy turned towards him.

'The next few weeks?' she protested in despair. 'I can't—I...'

'The name of your hotel?' Luke repeated.

Her lips numb, Suzy told him. Luke watched her in silence.

'Right, we'll go there now and get your stuff.' He glanced at his watch. 'It will soon be dinner time, and that will be a perfect opportunity for me to introduce you. Which reminds me—you had better get used to calling me Luke.'

'Luke?' Suzy checked him, confused. 'But I thought your name was Lucas?'

'Officially, it is,' he agreed coolly. 'Lucas is an old family name, from my father's family, but my mother always called me Luke.' His expression shadowed a little, and against her will Suzy felt an emotional tug on her heartstrings. 'My friends call me Luke, and as my partner so must you.'

'As your partner…' Suzy began shakily. Her heart was thumping, and not solely because of the speed with which Luke was forcing her to walk down the hill alongside him.

'Partner as in living together. Partner as in lovers!' Luke answered calmly.

Lovers? Suzy heart jerked frantically. She couldn't. She wouldn't!

'I… Will I have my own room?' Suzy could hear the wobble in her voice.

Luke stood still and looked at her. What kind of game was she trying to play now? The Little Miss Innocent nervous act certainly didn't fool him, and he was surprised that she should try it.

'Of course you will have your own room,' he said silkily.

Suzy began to exhale in a rush.

'However, it will also be my room,' Luke informed her grimly. 'And let me warn you right now that I am a very light sleeper, and trained to wake at the slightest sound. If there's one thing I hate it's having my sleep disturbed, so if you were rash enough to try to leave the room during the night I warn you that I am not likely to react with either charity or gentleness. Do I make myself understood?'

Suzy lingered mentally over a handful of biting retorts before reluctantly abandoning in favour of safety and silence.

'And whilst we are on the subject I might as well point out to you that there are guards posted at every exit from the villa and my men patrol the grounds.

Trying not to look afraid, Suzy demanded, 'Won't it look odd for me to suddenly turn up at the villa? I mean, you're here on business, and you don't strike me as the kind of man who would allow his partner to just appear and expect...'

He was watching her with a narrow-eyed intensity that unnerved her.

'We had a quarrel about how much time we have to spend apart before I left London,' Luke told her smoothly. 'You've realised how idiotic you were being and you've come here to apologise to me.'

'I was being idiotic?' Suzy stopped him wrathfully, her fear forgotten as she leapt to the defence of her sex. 'And now I'm apologising...?'

'Since I'm here on holiday with an old friend and his children—' Luke ignored her outburst '—what could be more natural than that you should join us?'

'You're here on holiday?' Suzy shook her head challengingly. 'I saw with my own eyes those men and that car and—'

'*You* may have seen them,' Luke said with cold menace, 'but I intend to make sure you do not get the opportunity to say so—to any-one. And most especially not to Roy Jarvis!'

'Why won't you accept that I do not work for the magazine any more?' Suzy demanded in frustration. 'And as for the men I saw—' She gave a dismissive shrug. 'I just saw them, that's all.'

'You just saw them? I saw you photo-graphing them,' Luke reminded her damn-ingly.

'Because I thought it would make a good photograph to show my friends. They run a holiday company,' Suzie told him in frustra-tion. 'Look, I can give you their name and phone number and you can ring them and—'

'Credit me with some intelligence.' Luke stopped her dryly. 'Of course Jarvis will have set up an alibi for you!'

'No. You can ring them now. Look, I've got my mobile,' Suzy insisted, putting her hand in her pocket to retrieve it.

Instantly Luke's hand clamped over her own. 'I'll take that, thank you,' he an-nounced, removing her hand from her pocket and then sliding his own into it to remove the phone.

The sensation of his hand pressing against her hipbone made her whole body burn. Warily, Suzy held her breath, exhaling with relief when Luke removed his hand, along with her phone.

But, to her shock, once he had transferred her mobile into his own possession he reached out and took hold of her hand as they approached the resort.

To anyone else they would look like a couple enjoying the warmth of the Italian sunshine, Suzy recognised. But of course they were no such thing. Experimentally she tried to remove her hand, wincing as she felt the crushing pressure of Luke's imprisoning response.

'Where is your hotel?' Luke asked.

He might be addressing her, but his gaze was measuring everything and everyone around them, Suzy saw as she glanced up at him. He was scanning the happy crowd of holidaymakers surrounding them.

Even in casual holiday clothes there was still an aura of command and authority about him. Suzy could see the way women's heads turned towards him, their glances lingering on him.

Had they really been a couple... A quiver of emotion ran through her.

'Where's your hotel?' Luke repeated, shooting her a cold, impatient look.

Suzy wondered wrathfully how she could allow herself to be vulnerable to a man like this. A man who could not recognise the truth when it and she were standing here beside him!

'It's here,' Suzy told him reluctantly, nodding in the direction of the drive which led up to the discreetly elegant boutique hotel where she was staying.

'You're staying here?'

She could see Luke frowning as though he was surprised.

'Where did you think I'd be staying?' Suzy taunted as they walked through the entrance, their progress noted by the sharp-eyed doorman who seemed instinctively to know who was resident at the hotel without having to check. 'Somewhere brash and flashy?'

'Well, that would certainly be more in keeping with your boss's tastes,' Luke agreed coolly.

They had reached the hotel now. Originally a private villa, it had only recently been converted and extended into its present form. A cool tiled hallway led into the reception area and the clerk on duty smiled at Suzy in recognition, reaching for her room key before she had to ask.

'I'll take that,' Luke announced, ignoring the clerk's uncertain look.

'Ms Roberts will be checking out as of now,' he informed him. 'Where's your passport?' he asked Suzy, turning to look at her.

If the clerk had thought originally that she was taking Luke back to her room so that they could make love, and Suzy suspected he must have done, he obviously did not think so now. Suzy saw his manner towards Luke change from uncertainty to respect.

But then there was quite definitely something about Luke that set him apart from other men, Suzy acknowledged grudgingly, angrily aware of his presence behind her as she walked to her room.

Her room—the room originally to have been provided for her friends—was elegant and extremely luxurious, with French doors which led out onto a private balcony large enough for her to have had a tea party on, had she so wished.

'Expensive,' was Luke's cynical comment as he followed her inside, and then locked the door and leaned against it, pocketing the old-fashioned key. If there had been an ounce of truth in her story that she was unemployed she could never have afforded to stay in a place like this, he acknowledged.

'But then I'm sure your boss has his own way of making sure he gets value for money.'

Angry heat burned Suzy's face as she started to open the wardrobe doors. Her whole body trembled in reaction to his taunt that she would have sex with a man she loathed! Unable to stop herself, she turned to confront Luke, pride and anger burning red flags in her small face.

'I know what you're trying to insinuate, but you couldn't be more wrong. You know nothing about me, and yet you think—'

'On the contrary. I know a good deal about you.' Luke stopped her smoothly. 'Everyone who attended the Prince's reception was vetted, including you.'

Vetted, yes, but he did not have an in-depth report on her, Luke acknowledged, and made a mental note to inform his staff in London that he required one—if only for formality's sake.

The intensity of her own emotions was exhausting her, and she just did not have the energy to argue with him any more, Suzy decided wearily.

'How long do you intend to keep me here in Italy?' she demanded as she opened her case and started to fold her clothes neatly.

'For as long as it takes,' Luke answered her laconically, his eyes narrowing as he focused on the clothes she was packing.

Neat round-necked tee shirts, modest pairs of walking shorts, a couple of long dresses—simple, anonymous clothes of a type he would have expected a conventional, rather cautions young woman to favour, hardly in keeping with the woman he knew her to be.

She had planned for her current role quite well, he acknowledged reluctantly as he watched the way she folded every garment before packing it.

Warily Suzy gave a glance in Luke's direction. He was still leaning against the bedroom door, arms folded, eyelids dropping over his eyes so that she couldn't be sure whether he was watching her or not.

She had packed virtually everything now, except her underwear, and for some ridiculous reason she discovered that she was reluctant to do so with him watching her.

She stole another glance at Luke.

'Finished?'

'Er, no…'

'Perhaps I'd better help you, then.'

Suzy's mouth opened and closed again as he levered his shoulders off the door and came towards her. Automatically she fell back, putting a protective hand on the drawer which contained her underwear.

She was trying to hide something from him, Luke recognised, his gaze narrowing on the betraying movement of her hand. What was it she had in the drawer that she didn't want him to see? He intended to find out.

'Have you got anything in the bathroom?' he asked casually. 'Toilet bag? Make-up?'

Unwittingly Suzy took the bait he had offered her. 'Yes...'

'You'd better go and get them, then, hadn't you?' Luke told her impatiently, glancing at his watch and informing her, 'You've got two minutes. After that, anything you haven't packed will have to be left behind.'

Automatically Suzy hurried to the bathroom.

The minute she was out of sight, Luke pulled open the drawer she had been guarding.

Neat piles of clean white underwear greeted his searching gaze.

Quickly and expertly he searched through it, frowning as his senses unwantedly relayed to him the cool, soft feel of the white fabric and its innocent virginal message.

Innocent? Virginal? Suzy Roberts?

She had researched her role well, he reflected, his frown deepening as he recognised that a part of him was reacting to the intimacy of what he was doing in a way that was both unprofessional and totally unfamiliar.

In his hand he held the semi-sheer white lace-trimmed bra he had just removed to check that the underwiring was just that.

He remembered with what ease and lack of any kind of sexual interest or arousal he had removed the TV news reporter's openly sexual underwear from the 'washing line' she had managed to delude one of the raw recruits into erecting for her. It seemed incomprehensible to him that he should be feeling such a fierce surge of sexual reaction now!

The sensation of his body beginning to strain against the constriction of his clothes had him ceasing his search to question what on earth his body thought it was doing.

Suzy, her toiletries packed, emerged from the bathroom and froze at the sight of Luke standing in front of the chest, one of her bras in his hand.

'What are you doing? How dare you touch my...my clothes?'

Like a small whirlwind, Suzy dropped her toiletries bag on the bed and snatched her bra from Luke's grasp, bundling it and as much of the other contents of the drawer as she could manage into her open case.

He had sent her into the bathroom deliberately so that he could go through her things! What in hell's name was happening to him? Luke wondered in disbelief as her angry, almost anguished movements caused an unexpected and fierce resurgence of the erection he thought he had tamed.

Furious with himself for his physical response to her, he told her sharply, 'Forget the shocked virgin act—it doesn't work. It stopped working for any woman over eighteen years ago, and when it comes to a woman like you…'

What would he do if she turned round now and told him just how wrong he was? Suzy wondered bitterly as her hands trembled over her final packing. But of course she already knew, didn't she? He simply would not believe her. He would not accept that her experience was limited to one fumbling incident whilst at university, in which she and her partner had both lost their virginity. Their relationship had ended with no regrets on either part when she had decided to give up her studies to nurse her mother…

'Time's up,' Luke announced tersely.

Another minute in this room, with its huge bed and her scent lying on the warm afternoon air, and he was not sure…

He was not sure what? Luke questioned himself brutally.

His body gave him an answer his professionalism wanted to deny.

He wasn't sure he wouldn't be able to stop himself from spreading her on that bed and...

Ignoring the savage ache in his groin, Luke searched the room silently, checking every drawer and cupboard and even looking under the bed and on top of the wardrobe before reaching for Suzy's suitcase.

CHAPTER FIVE

'COME on—and remember I shall be watching your every step and your every word. One move out of line and you'll be in an Italian prison faster than you can take another breath,' Luke warned Suzy as they stood in the late-afternoon sunshine of the villa's impressive forecourt, with the villa itself behind them and Suzy's case at Luke's feet. Any chance she might have had of escaping disappeared, as their taxi drove away.

'You will never be able to get away with this,' Suzy warned him angrily. 'Someone is bound to suspect...'

'If by "someone" you mean Sir Peter Verey, then I'm afraid you're going to be disappointed. He's far too busy trying to cope with his children,' Luke told her grimly.

'What do you mean "cope with his children"?' Suzy demanded.

Luke's comment had all the hallmarks of the kind of old-fashioned attitude towards parenting which she personally deplored.

'Why shouldn't he look after them? If his wife—'

Luke looked at her, well aware of her antagonism.

'Their mother is actually his ex-wife. She left him for someone much richer! And as for looking after his children... They are probably more capable of looking after him than the other way around,' Luke announced dryly. 'Peter is the product of a typical upper-class upbringing and totally incapable of any kind of hands-on parenting.'

Luke's grim words evoked Suzy's immediate sympathy on behalf of the two children. She too had had a parent—her mother, in her case—who had not been able to provide her with strong and loving parenting.

Suzy's eyes darkened as she became lost in her thoughts. Her mother had never really got over being widowed, and even before her health had begun to fail Suzy had found herself as a very young girl taking on the role of 'mothering' her own mother.

Her sympathies aroused on behalf of the children, she demanded, 'Why are they here, then? Or can I guess?' she asked angrily. 'I suppose you organised it for some machiavellian reason of your own. Have you no feelings? Don't you realise how much harm it could do them, to be here under such circumstances? Doesn't their mother—'

Luke listened to her passionate outburst in silence. What would she say if he were to tell her that he himself had been orphaned at a young age? Would that fiercely passionate championship he could see in her eyes for Peter Verey's children be there for the child he had been?

'Children are so vulnerable,' Suzy railed furiously. 'Surely their mother...'

Children are so vulnerable. Luke looked away from her, momentarily forgetting who she was. There was a bitter taste in his mouth and his gaze was clouded by painful memories.

Some children—as he had good cause to know—were more vulnerable than others. Abruptly inside his head images he didn't want to relive were starting to form. He banished them. They belonged to the past, and right now he needed to concentrate on the present.

'Their mother is more interested in scoring points against their father than concerning herself about the children they created together. She has a new partner now, who has no intention of playing happy families with them, so the children have become both a means of remaining a thorn in her ex-husband's side, and a punishment, because she now sees them as a burden she is forced to bear. She's put them both into boarding school, and it seems that the summer holidays and the departure of the girl she employed to take charge of them means their presence is a nuisance. Hence her decision to send them to their father. Conveniently, the day she informed Sir Peter he had to take charge of them was also the day she left on an extended holiday with her second husband.'

As she saw the anger in Luke's eyes Suzy immediately jumped to the wrong conclusion. It was obvious that he too considered the poor children to be an unwanted nuisance, she decided angrily—an inconvenience to mar his plans, just like her!

'Of course you don't want them here any more than their father,' she accused him.

'I don't want them here,' Luke agreed grimly.

He didn't want any child ever again to be anywhere it might be in danger, no matter how small that risk might be.

If he closed his eyes now Luke knew he would see the most terrible images of carnage and destruction etched in fire and blood. Images he would never be able to forget.

The situation here was dangerously volatile. The African President had a reputation for seeing threats round every corner and reacting punishingly to them. Violence was a way of life to him, and to his followers.

A simple mission, MI5 had called it. But how could it possibly be simple with a woman like Suzy Roberts and two innocent children involved?

'Come on,' Luke commanded, picking up Suzy's case. 'And remember, take one step just one centimetre over the line and you'll be locked up in jail before you can take another.'

He meant it Suzy recognised apprehensively, and she fought not to back away from him and let him know how much he was intimidating her.

'We're lovers, remember?' Luke warned her, closing the gap between them.

Ignoring the lynx-eyed look he was giving her, Suzy took a deep breath. Lovers! Panic shot through her as she recognised that her instinctive response to the thought was not one of abhorrence and rejection. Why wasn't it? She wasn't still holding onto that idiotic thing about them being soul mates, was she?

Lovers! Inside her head images were forming. Dangerous, wanton and tormenting images that made her body ache and burn.

Beneath her thin top Suzy could feel her nipples stiffening and peaking. Her heart thudding erratically, she turned away from him to look up at the villa. It was awesomely elegant and magnificent.

'Built by an Italian prince for his favourite mistress and the children she had by him,' Lucas informed her. 'The frescoes around the hall and staircase include images of both her and their sons. Come on.'

The visually gentle clasp of his hand around hers was in reality anything but, Suzy recognised and she flinched beneath his tight grip.

'My things—' she began, but Luke shook his head.

'I'll get someone to come out for them.'

The supposed butler who opened the door to them exchanged a look with Luke which made her suspect that the man was more than just a servant. One of Luke's men? Suzy suspected so, but before she could voice her suspicions one of the doors off the hallway opened and a young boy of around six came running out, hotly pursued by a pre-teenage girl who was protesting crossly,

'That's mine, Charlie, give it back to me now.'

'Children! Oh—Luke.'

This must be the children's father, Suzy guessed, and she waited to be introduced to her unsuspecting host.

He was tall and good-looking, with crinkly blue eyes and a nice smile, but Suzy still recognised that of the two of them it was obvious that Luke was the one in charge.

'Peter, I am delighted to tell you that you have an additional guest,' Luke announced. 'My partner, Suzy Roberts. Darling, this is Sir Peter Verey,'

'Luke, I applaud your taste.' Peter Verey smiled warmly, his words for Luke but his admiring gaze fixed very firmly on Suzy.

There was something almost endearing about Peter Verey, Suzy decided as she tried rebelliously to move away from Luke, but then tensed as his fingers closed around her wrist in steely warning.

'I'm going to take Suzy up to my room. It's almost dinnertime…'

Suzy opened her mouth to say something, but Luke took immediate action to forestall her by the simple expedient of silencing her protest with the pressure of his mouth on her own.

Caught like a rabbit in a car's headlights, she stared up into his eyes and saw the warning glinting there. But the warning certainly didn't match the soft, sensual pressure of his mouth as it moved on hers, Suzy recognised as her heart thumped painfully. He was holding her, kissing her as though…

A huge lump formed in her throat and she had to close her eyes against the sharp pain that speared her heart. As she did so she felt him lifting his mouth from hers.

They were alone in the vast hallway, Sir Peter having discreetly disappeared.

'This way,' Luke announced curtly.

He had released her wrist and Suzy noticed that he made no attempt to re-imprison her. In fact as she walked numbly towards the stairs he seemed to deliberately hang back a little from her. The lump in her throat turned to icy panic as she realised how bereft her body felt at its lack of contact with him.

He was a monster. She ought to hate and loathe him. She *did* hate and loathe him. It was just her body that was vulnerable to him. That was all.

Stopping mid-step, she turned on the stair and looked at Luke. He was two stairs below her and their eyes were on the same level. As she looked into his her heart gave a funny little kick-beat before flinging itself at the wall of her chest.

'Do we really have to share a room?' she asked, anxiety thickening her voice to a husky whisper.

Something in the soft timbre of her voice was touching a nerve he didn't want to have touched, Luke recognised angrily—arousing a reaction he didn't want to have aroused. What the devil was the matter with him?

'Yes, because that will ensure that I can keep a very close eye on you, and it will reinforce the necessary fiction I've had to create that we are lovers,' Luke said to her prosaically, adding scathingly, 'I should have thought you could have worked that out for yourself. I assure you there's no other reason for it.'

Mutely Suzy looked at him, then turned away and began to climb the remaining stairs.

What was it about those eyes that made him want to take hold of her?

Infuriated by the effect Suzy was having on him, Luke followed her up the stairs.

'This way.' Tensing beneath Luke's brief touch on her bare arm, Suzy willed herself not to betray how emotionally vulnerable he was making her feel.

He had come to a halt outside a door which he unlocked and pushed open.

Warily Suzy stepped inside, her eyes widening as she took in the magnificence of her surroundings.

What she was standing in wasn't just a room but a suite. Almost an apartment, she decided, and she gazed around in awe, recognising wryly that her own small flat would have fitted easily into the elegant and spaciously proportioned sitting room in which she was now standing. Through the three tall windows she could see the grounds of the villa, but it wasn't the view from the windows that caught and held her attention. As she stared through the double doors which opened into what was obviously the bedroom Suzy felt her throat constrict.

Because she could see that the bedroom did in fact possess only one bed. A very large bed, admittedly, but still only one.

'I am not sleeping in that bed with you,' she announced flatly.

She looked and sounded shocked and outraged, Luke recognised. Pink flags of apparent distress were flying in her cheeks and her eyes were glittering with emotion. Even her body language, her tightly balled fists and tensely held body, was perfect for the part she had chosen to play.

She was good, he told himself angrily. She was very, very good. But he wasn't fooled!

'Well, you certainly won't be doing anything other than sleeping!' he told her emphatically. 'So you can disabuse yourself of any ideas you might be entertaining of favouring me with your sexual expertise. Because I'm not in the market for it.'

Somewhere inside her a small, sensible voice was trying to make itself heard, to tell her that she ought to be relieved by his words and the message of safety they held for her. But it was being drowned out by the outraged protests of her emotions, Suzy knew, and she recoiled from the rejection in Luke's words.

'I am not going to sleep with you!'

Could he hear the panic in her voice? Suzy no longer cared. All she cared about was saving herself from the humiliation of having to share a bed with a man she already knew had the most dangerous effect on her body—especially when he had made it so clear how he felt about her. She could not, *would* not share Luke's bed!

Was it because she was afraid that if she did she might somehow forget herself and…?

And what? Suzy derided herself mirthlessly. Seduce him? Her? Seduce a man like Luke?

'I'll sleep in the sitting room on one of the sofas,' she announced shakily.

'No!' Luke checked her immediately.

The cool word offered no hope of a compromise.

Uncertainly Suzy looked at him.

'Didn't you listen to what I told you?' he asked softly. 'I am not going to let you out of my sight! Night and day, wherever I go, you come with me. Besides, we are supposed to be lovers. I don't want the maids gossiping that we aren't sleeping together. Of course, if you prefer to spend the next few weeks in prison...' he offered cordially.

There was a cold look in his eyes that told her he wasn't joking. Wildly Suzy contemplated telling him that she *would* prefer the option of prison. Surely anything was better than having to share his bed! Than lying there beside him, terrified that she might somehow be overwhelmed by temptation and reach out to him and be rejected.

'The bathroom's through here,' she heard Luke informing her, quite obviously waiting for her to follow him.

A small spurt of rebellion surged through her. Suzy stayed where she was.

Luke paused and turned to look at her. 'Are you waiting for me to come and get you?' he asked softly.

Silently they looked at one another.

Something unseen and dangerous sizzled in the air between them. Suzy might not be able to see it, but she could certainly feel it. Inside she was trembling, teetering on a tight-rope of hyped-up sexual excitement and over-stretched emotions.

If she stayed here what would Luke do? Just the thought of his hands on her body in any kind of way sent a high-voltage shock of sensual longing jolting through her.

What was happening to her?

Gritting her teeth, she took a step towards him. Anything, even giving in to him now, was a million times better than putting herself in a position where she might humiliate herself by letting Luke see...

See what? What was there to see? she asked herself with angry defiance. But of course she knew!

How on earth could she be unlucky enough to have the kind of emotional and sexual feelings she did towards a man like Luke? And why, knowing what he thought of her, hadn't she been able to destroy them?

And, as if that wasn't enough for her to have to cope with, why had fate deemed it necessary to condemn her to this current situation, where she would be exposed day and night to Luke's proximity? Day and night!

Luke frowned as he watched the expressions chase one another over Suzy's face. That look of agonised despair he had just seen darken her eyes had surely been pure theatre!

Numbly Suzy followed Luke into the bathroom, then stopped dead to stare in disbelief and bemusement around the room.

'The current owner renovated the whole place, with particular attention to the bathrooms,' she heard Luke explaining calmly while she stood and stared, then turned and closed her eyes, and then opened them again.

The bathroom was like something out of a private fantasy!

The bath was huge, round and half-sunk into the floor. It was dark green marble with marble steps leading down to it and gold dolphin-head taps attached.

As though that were not enough five columns surrounded it, supporting a cupola-type canopy the centre of which was painted with…Suzy blinked, and then blinked again at the scenes of extremely explicit sensuality above her head. And not just above her head, she realised, but all along the wall frieze as well! Luscious-breasted women, each with her godlike Adonis entwined in a variety of intimate sexual embraces! Huge mirrors covered one of the walls, and on another she could see handbasins…

'I...' she began falteringly, shaking her head when her voice failed her and her gaze was drawn back to the frieze!

Hastily she refocused it on the bathtub, and then wished she had not as, out of nowhere, the most intimate and erotic images presented themselves to her.

Luke sleekly wet and naked... Luke bending over her as one Adonis on the frieze was bending over his lover...

A dizzying surge of sensual heat gripped her body. Fiercely she tried to repel it.

Luke himself, who had previously derided and then ignored the flamboyantly sensual décor of the bathroom, had a sudden and unwanted image of Suzy lying in the ornate tub, her naked body gleaming with pearly iridescence. Would the tangle of curls between her thighs be the same unique shade of gold as her hair? And when he lifted her out of the water and laid her down, so that he could caress the taut peaks of her breasts with his fingers, before he touched her more intimately, would those curls cling lovingly to his fingers as he parted the folded lips of her sex?

Furious with himself, Luke turned away from Suzy to stop her from seeing the effect his thoughts were having on him. His erection was straining against his clothes and throbbing almost painfully. The physical rebelliousness of his body was a hazard he had not accounted for, never having had to deal with it before, and mentally Luke cursed that unexpected kiss Suzy had given him the first time they had met.

Then she had caught him off guard, and somehow superimposed on his body and his arousal mechanism an imprinted response to her which right now he seemed powerless to destroy!

'The shower is over there,' he told Suzy curtly, breaking off as they both heard a discreet knock on the outside door to the suite. 'That will be your stuff.'

Glad of a reason to escape from the overwhelming sensuality of the bathroom, Suzy hurried back into the suite, Luke at her heels.

A young Italian was standing beside the door with Suzy's case. As Suzy thanked him he gave her an intense and admiring look.

'I'll take that,' Luke announced tersely, somehow managing to insert himself between Suzy and the young man as he dismissed him. 'You've got half an hour before dinner,' he told Suzy as he closed the door, shutting her inside the suite, on her own with him. 'I've only used part of the wardrobe, so you'll have plenty of space for your stuff.'

Her stuff? It was just as well that the exclusivity of her hotel meant that she had brought a couple of outfits with her more formal than she would normally have packed for a holiday, Suzy acknowledged.

'You can use the shower first if you like.'

'Yes, thanks—I will,' she told him woodenly, unzipping her case and trying to be discreet as she extracted clean underwear. But it was next to impossible when Luke was standing right next to her.

'If you need anything pressing now's the time to say,' he told her, ignoring her discomfort.

'Well, what kind of thing should I wear? I mean, how formal...?' she began uncertainly. Something told her that Sir Peter Verey was not someone who sat down to dinner wearing a pair of jeans!

'Will these be okay?' she asked reluctantly, removing a pair of linen trousers from her case. She hated to have to ask him for anything, even a small piece of advice, but she knew that she had no choice.

'They won't need pressing,' she told him, and he nodded his head.

Quickly hanging them up, she found her toilet bag and headed for the bathroom. As she did so she thought she heard Luke call something after her, but she refused to turn back to find out what it was. Another criticism of her, no doubt, she decided, and she closed the bathroom door with a satisfying bang.

Fortunately the shower was modern and plain, and no way in danger of inclining her toward wanton thoughts concerning her jailer!

Determinedly Suzy pushed away her dangerous fantasies and turned on the shower, carefully adjusting the heat and letting the water run for a few seconds before testing it to make sure the temperature was right.

Quickly stripping off her clothes, she stepped into it, enjoying the warm cascade of water over her skin. The warmth of the water was just perfect.

'Aaagrh!' Suzy screamed as suddenly icy cold water pelted her unprepared skin. Frozen, she reached for the towel she had hung over the shower door, but felt it slip from her grasp. It only took her seconds to escape from the shower's icy blast, but by the time she had she was shivering with cold and shock.

'I tried to warn you about the water but you didn't bother to listen.'

Soaking wet, shivering and totally naked, she stared in affronted outrage at Luke, who was standing in the doorway, having heard her scream and guessed its cause.

CHAPTER SIX

'HERE.' In two quick strides Luke was beside her, having grabbed hold of a towel.

'No, don't—I can manage.' She began to protest, but the words became a muddled muffle as he wrapped her unceremoniously in the towel and started to rub her dry so fiercely that her skin began to glow.

His actions were spare, rigorous and practical, and there was no reason at all why they should remind her of the loving care of her mother when she was a little girl, but they did. And then she turned her head and stiffened as she saw the way he was looking at her. He had stopped towelling her, and what she could see in his eyes was making her heart turn over and her resistance melt.

Frantically she forced herself to remember who he was and what he had done! Glaring at him, she turned away and headed for the bedroom, only to give a gasp of shock as she tripped on the hem of her towel.

The speed with which Luke moved was very impressive. One minute he was standing beside her, the next he was catching her in his arms and swinging her up off the floor, so that instead of taking a nasty tumble she was held securely against his warm chest.

Initially she struggled to break free, then suddenly the whole world stopped turning and her heartbeat was suspended with it.

'Luke…'

She had barely whispered his name, but he must have heard her because she could feel him registering it. His body tensed, as though there was something in her one little word that he needed every bit of his formidable artillery of weaponry to repel.

'I just don't need this,' Suzy heard him mutter savagely, but then his hand was pushing through her hair, securing her head at just the right angle for his mouth to home in on hers, to take it and make her want to return the passion she could feel in his kiss. It was the same passion that was running through her like liquid fire and honey. Any thought of resisting him or of denying herself the pleasure her body craved was forgotten!

She lifted up her arms and put them round him. This time it was *her* tongue-tip that probed the line of *his* lips, but it was Luke who drew it deep inside the dark, warm sensuality of his mouth, coaxing it, encouraging it, and then fiercely mating with it. Her heart was bouncing around inside her chest like a yo-yo. She could hardly breathe—and not just because of the way Luke was kissing her.

Like a snake sloughing off an unwanted skin, she wriggled her body until the towel dropped off, her action driven by instinct and not any deliberate thought. She was incapable of that! Incapable of anything other than responding to the subtle pressure of Luke's hard hand holding her head, Luke's equally hard mouth on hers.

His hands were on her naked back, splaying out against her skin, sliding downwards to her waist and then her buttocks, cupping their rounded softness and then pulling her fiercely into his own body, his own arousal. Helpless to stop herself, Suzy ground her hips against him.

What he was doing was crazy, Luke warned himself. He must be out of his mind for even thinking about contemplating what he was contemplating. If he had any sense he would back off right now and—

He felt Suzy's body move against his own, heard the soft, hot sound of excitement she made against his skin and his aroused body refused to obey his demands. He lifted his hand to cover her naked breast, feeling the taut nub push eagerly against his palm.

Suddenly Suzy realised what she was doing. With a small moan of anguish she pushed at Luke's chest.

Immediately he set her free. His face was hard with anger and her own face felt tight with shock and misery.

Unsteadily Suzy retrieved her towel, dreading what Luke might be going to say. Had he guessed what he had done to her?

How he had made her feel? How he had made her want him?

To her relief he strode towards the bathroom without saying anything, leaving her alone to dress.

In the bathroom Luke fought furiously to sandbag his feelings. How could he have allowed himself to react to her like that—to respond to her like that? He tried to pinpoint the second things had got out of control, and the reason, rerunning the whole thing through his head in order to reexamine it and sort out some kind of damage limitation plan. But to his disbelief he realised that remembering how Suzy had looked standing there naked was already arousing him again.

Turning on the shower, Luke stepped under its icy blast, savagely angry with himself and equally angry with Suzy. Did she really think he had been deceived by the role she was trying to play, or by the white-faced look of despair he had seen in her eyes as she tore herself out of his arms?

As she tore herself out of his arms. The icy jets of water needled onto Luke's skin unnoticed as he stood still.

Suzy had been the one to end their intimacy, not him, and if she had not done so by now she would be lying beneath his body.

Cursing himself Luke tried to ignore the images his mind was relaying to him. He was a man who intended to live his life to a specific moral code; she was a woman who didn't have a moral bone in her body! An impossible coupling! And he intended to ensure that it remained impossible!

'Ready?'

Numbly Suzy nodded her head, not trusting herself to speak.

She was wearing a simple linen top with shoestring straps with her trousers, and Luke frowned as he looked at her, recognising how effective the outfit was at making her appear fragile and somehow vulnerable.

As he opened the suite door for her Suzy snatched a brief look at Luke, helplessly aware that the sight of him, in a pair of immaculate dark-coloured trousers and an equally immaculate soft white shirt, was doing things to her she had no wish whatsoever to acknowledge.

As they descended the impressive staircase together, Suzy was acutely conscious of him at her side. When they reached the hallway he touched her bare arm lightly, and immediately she flinched.

'We're a couple, remember?' Luke warned her in a low, cold voice.

As he reached past her to push open the door Suzy caught the clean male smell of his skin, and immediately a quiver of response ran down her spine. She felt an overwhelming urge to turn round and bury her face in his throat, just breathe in the smell of him until she was drunk on it.

'In here!'

The door opened and Suzy stepped through it, Luke behind her. The two children she had seen earlier were seated on a windowseat, their heads bent over a computer game. Suzy felt an unexpected tug of emotion as she saw that, despite their clean clothes, they somehow had a heart-rending air of neglect about them.

Was it because of her own childhood she was so immediately and instinctively aware that these children lacked a mother's loving input into their lives? Suzy wondered ruefully as she watched them.

Sir Peter was picking up the drink which had just been poured for him by the smartly dressed waiter. As he saw them he put it down.

'There you are! Suzy, my dear, what will you have to drink, Luke, are you going to break your normal abstinence tonight?'

For all that he was their host, Suzy could see that Sir Peter was actually a little in awe of Luke, and she watched the interaction between the two men curiously as Luke announced that he would simply have a tonic.

'And Suzy?' Sir Peter pressed, giving her another warm smile.

'Tonic for me too,' she echoed.

'I'm afraid we have to let the children have dinner with us,' Sir Peter apologised to Suzy as the young Italian waiter handed her her drink. 'It really is a nuisance having them here, but I'm afraid I wasn't given the opportunity to refuse.'

A heavy sigh accompanied the frowning look Sir Peter gave his children, and Suzy's sympathy for them increased.

'Perhaps I should go and introduce myself to them,' she suggested gently, leaving Luke standing with Sir Peter whilst she made her way over to the windowseat.

As Suzy walked away Luke discovered that his gaze was focused on the gentle sway of her hips and the rounded curves of her bottom.

'Lovely girl,' he heard Peter saying appreciatively at his side. 'I envy you, old chap.'

Luke saw that the other man's gaze was lingering on Suzy's curvy posterior as well.

For no reason he could think of Luke moved to block his view.

'I wish we could hear definitely that our chap is going to come through...' Peter was complaining, and automatically Luke turned his attention to what he was saying.

'Hello, I'm Suzy.' Suzy introduced herself to the children with a smile.

'You're Lucas's girlfriend, aren't you?' the little boy demanded, adding importantly, 'Maria told us. She's one of the maids.'

Luke's girlfriend! Something turned over inside Suzy's chest, and an odd and unwanted feeling of loss and pain ached inside her.

'Charlie, you shouldn't gossip with the servants. Mummy wouldn't like it,' the little girl announced primly, and Suzy could see the mixture of anxiety and protectiveness in her eyes as she looked at her younger brother.

'You can't tell me what to do, Lucy,' He retaliated immediately. 'Does being Luke's girlfriend mean that you are going to get married?' he asked Suzy.

Married! To Luke!

A feeling of fierce intensity shot through her.

'Charlie, it's rude to ask personal questions,' Lucy told him imperiously.

'Our mother and father were married,' Charlie told her, ignoring his sister, 'but they aren't any more. Our mother is married to someone else, and he doesn't like us, does he, Lucy?'

'Charlie, you aren't supposed to say things like that,' Lucy hissed, red-faced.

'Why not? I heard Mummy saying it to Aunt Catherine.'

Poor children, Suzy thought sadly. Charlie was still too young to be aware of what he was saying, but Lucy was old enough to be embarrassed and upset by her younger brother's revelations. Suzy could see that, so she gently distracted them, asking, 'What was that game I saw you playing?'

Her simple ploy had the desired effect. Immediately Charlie began to enthuse about the game and his skill with it.

As she listened to him Suzy turned to look at Lucy. The little girl gave her a hesitant smile. The pristinely laundered dress she was wearing, whilst unmistakably expensive, was too short and too tight, Suzy recognised, and she wondered absently if she had perhaps chosen to wear it because it was an old favourite.

Still listening to Peter complaining about the way the visiting Head of State kept changing the carefully made arrangements, Luke looked towards the window.

The children were now seated either side of Suzy, apparently hanging onto her every word—nestling against her, almost.

For some absurd reason the sight of the three of them together aroused an emotion inside him he wasn't prepared to name, and it was with relief that he heard the sound of the dinner gong.

'Suzy, my dear, you don't know what a pleasure it is for me to have the company of such a very attractive and charming young woman,' Sir Peter announced flatteringly once they were all seated around the magnificent antique table. 'And I'm sure the children agree with me—don't you, children?'

Obediently Charlie and Lucy nodded their heads.

'Luke, you are an extremely fortunate man. I just hope, Suzy, that we will be able to persuade you to spend some time with us as well as with Luke. The children would certainly welcome your company, I know.'

Suzy hid a smile as she realised what Sir Peter was trying to do. He obviously saw in her arrival an opportunity to persuade her into helping out with his children. And to be honest, she acknowledged, she would be perfectly happy to do so. It would give her something to occupy her time during her enforced imprisonment.

With that in mind, she smiled compliantly at her host.

'You must take Suzy for a walk through the gardens after dinner, Luke,' Sir Peter announced amiably, after giving Suzy a warmly approving smile. 'The grounds to the villa are very beautiful. There's a lake—'

'And a grotto,' Charlie broke in eagerly. 'I want to explore it.'

Immediately his father gave him a stern look. 'Charlie, I've already told you that you are not to go near the grotto. It's unsafe and too dangerous, and that's why a metal gate has been placed across it—it's too dangerous for anyone to enter!' Turning to Suzy, he told her, 'There is supposed to be some sort of tunnel and an underground chamber beneath the grotto, which was built originally as a folly.'

Suzy shivered as she listened to him. She had always had a fear of such places, and certainly did not share Charlie's enthusiasm.

'But you must show Suzy the sunken garden, Luke. It's a very romantic walk, Suzy,' he added warmly, 'and if Luke hadn't bagged you first, I can assure you I would have enjoyed showing it to you myself.'

Sir Peter was flirting with her!

Hastily Suzy took a sip of her wine, and then choked a little as she realised how strong it was.

The food was delicious, but she seemed to have lost her usual appetite, Suzy acknowledged as her churning stomach prevented her from eating more than a few mouthfuls of her meal.

Was it because every minute that passed meant that it was getting closer to the time when she would have to go back upstairs with Luke to that suite? Their suite. Their bed.

A tense shudder ripped through her and she reached for her wine again, hoping to distract herself.

The children were looking tired and had started bickering. It was far too late for them to be eating, in Suzy's opinion, and the food was surely too rich for young digestion.

'Charlie, that's enough!'

Peter was giving his son an angry look, but Suzy could see that the little boy's behaviour was caused more by tiredness than wilfulness.

'Finish your dinner,' Sir Peter instructed.

'I don't want it. I don't like it.' Charlie resisted stubbornly.

'Charles!'

'I think the children are tired,' Suzy intervened gently. 'It is rather late. I don't know what time they normally go to bed...'

'Of course. You are quite right! It *is* late!' Sir Peter agreed immediately. 'I'd better send for one of the maids to take them upstairs and put them to bed,' he added, signalling to the hovering waiter.

Within minutes a plump, elderly woman appeared, and their father instructed the children to go with her.

A small frown creased Suzy's forehead as both children followed the maid without receiving a goodnight kiss from their father.

Half an hour later, their own meal over, Suzy was beginning to feel tired herself—and to regret the two glasses of red wine she had drunk!

Coffee was to be served in the same salon where they had had their pre-dinner cocktails, and once they had made their way there Sir

Peter settled himself on one of the damask sofas. Patting the space beside himself, he invited, 'Come and sit here, next to me, Suzy, and tell me all about yourself.'

Hesitantly Suzy began to walk towards him, only to come to an unsteady stop as Luke stepped in front of her.

'If you don't mind, Peter, I think I'd like to have her to myself for a while,' he announced smoothly, taking hold of Suzy's arm as he did so.

Just the feel of his fingers on her bare arm was enough to make her quiver from head to foot, Suzy recognised dizzily.

'Of course, of course. Don't blame you, old chap,' Sir Peter responded heartily.

Before she could say or do anything Suzy discovered that she was being almost force-marched in the direction of the salon door. She could almost feel the blast of heat from Luke's anger as he opened the door and propelled her out into the hallway, up the stairs and into their suite.

As soon as he had closed the door behind them he rounded on her, demanding savagely, 'What the devil do you think you are playing at? Or do I need to ask? It's the same old trick, isn't it? I warned you—'

'I'm not playing at anything!' Suzy denied fiercely.

'Liar! You've seen that Peter is susceptible to you, so you're doing everything you can to encourage him...giving him limpid-eyed looks, pretending to be concerned about his children—'

'I *am* concerned about them!' Suzy stopped him. 'And as for me encouraging him—I was doing no such thing! You're behaving like a jealous lover!' she threw furiously at him. 'Accusing me of things I haven't done, and have no intention of doing!'

A jealous lover! Luke stared at her.

Suzy gasped as she was dragged into Luke's arms. She tried to protest. And she tried to resist. But the wine had obviously weakened her resistance. Of its own accord her hand clutched at the sleeve of his shirt and her body leaned into his. Greedily her senses absorbed the feel of him. Tough, male, strong... She looked at his mouth. She looked into his eyes. And then she looked at his mouth again. She could feel the sound he was making in his throat vibrate through his body in a feral growl of warning male arousal.

He was lowering his head and she wanted to reach up and hold it, so that he couldn't escape, so that his mouth had to cover her own...

And it did! How long had she yearned for this? Suzy wondered dizzily as her lips clung to his. Surrounded by the sensual soft dark of the Italian night, she gave in to her own need. She was in his arms and then in his hands—quite literally, she realised in soaring shocked pleasure as they moved over her, shaping her, learning her...

Into the darkness of their room she moaned her uninhibited delight. She could feel her breasts swelling into his hands whilst her stomach tightened with expectation. She lifted her arms to wrap them around him, her fingers sliding into the softness of his hair. His mouth tasted erotically of wine and man, and she wanted to feed on it until all her senses were sated with the pleasure of him. The straps of her top had slipped down her arms and were digging into her flesh, and she wanted to beg Luke to remove it from her body, right here and right now.

Helplessly Luke gave in to the need he had felt the first time she had kissed him. Then he had denied it, buried it, but somehow it had survived, tormenting him in his dreams. Luke felt his body shudder as his hunger for her ripped through his defences. Now he was beyond reason, beyond sanity, beyond anything and everything but wanting her. He was, Luke recognised distantly, completely out of control. And she was the one who had done this to him, who had driven him, aroused him, made him so insane with need for her. That eager female sound she had just made had logged straight into his body and switched on every damn thing, sending him completely crazy. He lifted his hand to push Suzy's auburn hair off her creamy neck and shoulder, leaving them exposed to the exploration of his hungry mouth. A tiny pulse jumped and skittered beneath his kiss and he paused to touch it with his tongue.

She was openly trembling with longing, Suzy recognised as her head fell back to allow Luke even more access to the curve of her throat. Behind her she had the hardness of the heavy wooden door, and in front of her she had the hardness that was Luke. A deep shudder tormented her as he started to explore the delicate whorls of her ear, his thumb on the pulse at the base of her throat.

Someone was tugging frantically at the straps of her top trying to remove it. How could Luke be doing that and touching her as well?

It wasn't Luke who was tearing off her clothes and exhaling in a rush of fierce pleasure as they fell to the ground, Suzy realised. It was her.

Luke had felt her clothes slither to the floor as his eyes adjusted to the velvet darkness, and now he could see the pale outline of her body. Her almost naked body.

He had known that she wasn't wearing a bra—had known it and registered Peter's equal awareness of that fact—but that knowledge and the knowledge he had now, of the soft, pure nakedness of her torso, with the outline of her breasts sketched in blurred charcoal light, were a world apart.

Almost as though it was happening in slow motion Suzy watched as Luke turned his head and looked down at her body. His hand came out and slid beneath one breast, gently supporting it.

If she was any more perfect she wouldn't be human, Luke thought as he felt the delicious weight of Suzy's breast on his palm. His thumb searched for her nipple.

She gave a sharp, electrified moan and her whole body stiffened in response to his touch.

She was a conniving, manipulative wanton who had never had a genuine emotion or reaction in her life, Luke told himself savagely. But his body was beyond listening. His hand was working urgently on her breast, preparing it for the hungry possession of his mouth. Every sweet moan she made was causing the sensation in the pit of his belly to screw down harder. If he didn't have the taste of her in his mouth soon he was going to…

His free hand slid down her body and encountered the lacy edge of her underwear. He hooked one finger under what he thought was elastic and then realised that it was a ribbon bow. A bow he could untie with his fingers, or…Luke had a sudden mental picture of himself laying her on the bed, tugging the bows loose with his teeth. He wanted to eat her like a fresh peach, filling his mouth with her taste until the juice of her ran from his fingers and his lips.

His erection was straining against his clothes, and he could tell from the small urgent sounds Suzy was making that she was equally aroused.

They were partners, after all, he reminded himself with inner black humour. Partners on opposite sides of a very sharp divide, he acknowledged, and reality suddenly kicked in.

Suzy tensed as she felt Luke's hand start to leave her breast. Something had happened. Something had made him draw back from her, and she didn't want that something. She wanted *him*.

Suzy's sexual experience was relatively limited. And yet she discovered that her body knew far more than she had given it credit for. It knew, for instance, that if she reached out and touched Luke the way she was doing, just the merest brush of her fingertips, slowly, oh so slowly against that tight bulge she could feel beneath his clothing, that instead of pushing her away he would draw her to him again.

He shouldn't be doing this. Oh, he should not be doing this, Luke warned himself. But that provocative touch that Suzy was subjecting him to, just the slightest brush of delicate fingertips against his erection, was more than he could stand.

He wanted her right now.

He didn't just want to taste her, he wanted to take her and fill her and spill himself inside her.

Taking hold of her hands, Luke pinned them above her head, his body leaning into hers.

Her eyes had adjusted to the dark now, and Suzy could see his expression quite clearly. A fast, furious surge of shocked excitement raced through her. He had lost control now. She could see it in his eyes, feel it in the way he was grinding his body into hers—and she loved it...

As Luke felt Suzy's hips lift and writhe tormentingly against him he knew that there was no going back.

There was nothing he wanted more than to take her right here, against the damned door, as primitively as though every layer of civilisation had been stripped from them both. He wanted to hook his fingers in those ridiculous bows and leave himself free to give her every pleasure. He wanted to lift her up against him and have her wrap her legs around him whilst he buried himself so deep inside her that no other man would ever pleasure her as much.

Her fingers touched him again, and this time she was tracing his erection, gauging it—measuring it?

Suzy's chest tightened as her uncertain touch revealed to her just how much of a man Luke was! She could feel Luke lifting her up against him. Shocked pleasure surged through her on a riptide. He was going to make love to her here against the door!

She weighed next to nothing, Luke acknowledged as he lifted Suzy off the floor. The lacy thong she was wearing left the rounded contours of her bottom free to his touch. He could see the bright, aroused glitter of her eyes and he could feel the exhalation of her breath. His tongue touched her lips and then pierced her mouth. She tasted soft and sweet, warm and welcoming.

'Open your legs,' he commanded her.

Hot, urgent, immediate sex—that was what he wanted with her.

His hand was on his zip before he recognised that he wanted far more than that.

CHAPTER SEVEN

'WHAT are you doing?' Suzy protested as Luke suddenly swung her up into his arms. Had he changed his mind? Wasn't he going to make love to her after all? 'Why—?'

'Why?' He stopped her as he laid her on the bed. 'Because where we were would have been fine for a quickie,' he told her rawly. 'But right now I need to have much more than just that. Much, much more!' he said thickly, and brushed his lips against her half-parted mouth, then touched them to each nipple in turn before returning to her mouth to kiss her with deep ferocity.

Whilst he stripped off his clothes he told her what he wanted to do with her, how he wanted to touch her and how he wanted her to touch him. By the time he was fully nude Suzy was ready to explode. The heat in her lower body was unbearable, and so was the pressure.

Impulsively she reached down to remove her ribbon-tied thong.

'No!'

His hand was over hers, but instead of unfastening the bow he started to kiss her again. Her mouth, her shoulder, her breast, laving the tight peak until she was thrashing around beneath him. And then the other breast, taking his time whilst she cried out, her hands on his shoulders, her nails digging into his skin.

But that was nothing to what she felt when his mouth moved lower, his lips caressing her stomach and then his tongue rimming her navel, tracing the lacy edge of her thong from one bow to the other and then back again. She could feel his hands sliding beneath her, lifting her, and she writhed in urgent need. She felt his breath against her skin and watched in a sensual daze of arousal as he tugged at the bow with his teeth. When it came free he pressed his lips to her naked skin and his hand to her naked body, discovering, exploring, parting the swollen folds of flesh to expose her sex to his touch and his taste.

Suzy heard the sounds of pleasure flooding the room and knew they must be her own, but she had no awareness of having made them. She had no awareness of anything at all other than the touch of Luke's fingers and the lave of his tongue.

She felt the tightening warning of her body, but it was impossible for her to hold back her orgasm. As she cried out her pleasure she felt Luke's mouth taking it from her into his own keeping.

She was still trembling with its aftershock seconds later, when he moved up the bed to hold her, wrapping her tightly in his arms, his breath warm against the top of her head.

Was it because it had been such a long time since he had done this that her reaction had affected him so much? Luke questioned himself. Had he somehow forgotten just how intense the pleasure of pleasuring a woman was for him? Had he somehow managed to overlook the way it made him feel? Because he was damn sure that no one had given him this feeling before. Exhilarated, Suzy clung to Luke. His naked flesh felt smooth and warm beneath her fingertips. Idly she traced the line of his collarbone, and then pressed a small kiss to it for no other reason than that she wanted to. She ran her finger around the aureole of his nipple, dark and flat, unlike the rosy fullness of her own. The nipple itself was different too. She teased it languidly and then burrowed her face against his chest, relishing the scent and taste of him.

'If you keep doing that…' Luke warned her rawly.

'You'll do what?' Suzy challenged him deliberately.

'This,' he responded promptly, rolling her over and then beneath him.

Eagerly Suzy opened her legs and wrapped them round him, welcoming him into her soft warmth. Desire ran through her with liquid heat, but more than that, as her hips lifted and writhed and her body welcomed him with fierce female longing, Suzy recognised that it wasn't just her body that could feel him, that wanted him. It was her heart and her mind as well! And that meant—

But, no, she did not want to think about what that meant right now. In fact she did not want to think at all. She simply wanted to know. To experience. To feel. To be here in this place at this time with this man, and to hold on to what they were sharing for ever.

A sensation of exquisite urgency was filling her, taking her with him through time and space. Each thrust of his powerful body within her own brought them closer, physically and emotionally.

The increasingly fast movement of his thrusts was pushing her up the bed, and Suzy had to reach out to grab hold of the bedpost behind her.

In that same moment she heard his harsh cry, and felt again that same rainbow explosion within herself as she reached her climax, and it showered her whole body with quick silver darts of pleasure.

Soul mates. Meant to be together.

The words, the knowledge floated through her like precious stars set in a perfect sky.

As they lay in a damp and relaxed tumble of arms and legs, Suzy's head on his chest, his arms wrapped hard around her, Luke marvelled again at the intensity of his own pleasure. He had been so overwhelmed by his need for her that he hadn't even had time to think about any practicalities.

In his youth, when he had been as keen on exploring sex as any other teenager, he had practised safe sex—primarily because he had had no wish to become a father before he was ready. Over the last few years his career had meant that sex, safe or otherwise, simply wasn't on his personal agenda. But he had taken Suzy to bed without even taking the most rudimentary health precautions. She would be protected against pregnancy, of course, but it was a bit late now to demand a full report on her sexual health and history!

Moonlight streamed in through the window, leaving a silver trail on Luke's naked body. Suzy traced it with one loving finger, frowning as she suddenly found the hard ridge of a scar. Leaning up, she looked down at it, her heart twisting as she saw its raw newness. Overwhelmed by her feelings for him, she bent her head and tenderly placed her lips against the puckered ridge of flesh.

Immediately Luke tensed, wrenching himself away from her.

'What is it?' Suzy asked him in concern. 'Did I hurt you?'

When he shook his head she asked softly. 'How did it happen, Luke?' She couldn't bear to think of him being in danger, being hurt.

Pushing her away, Luke said harshly, 'If you must know it was caused by a woman just like you!'

He could see the shock in her face, but he ignored it.

'She may not have fired the bullet that caused it, but she was still responsible.'

A dark, frightening anger filled his expression, banishing the intimacy they had shared. Bitterly Luke contemplated what he had done. How could he not have controlled himself? Stopped himself? How could she have made him feel like that? How could she have made him want like that, when she was everything he did *not* want in a woman? Anger and self-disgust left a sour taste in his mouth.

'Luke?' Suzy whispered hesitantly.

Why wasn't he saying anything to her? Why was he turning away from her instead of holding her as she longed for him to do?

He had to make it plain to her that what had just happened between them hadn't left him vulnerable or open to any kind of persuasion, Luke told himself. He could still feel the soft warmth of her lips against his scar. Anger burned through him. A gunshot wound was nothing compared with what he could see inside his head. He saw the smouldering rubble of what had once been a home, the body of the pretty young woman who had lived in it lying on the ground like that of a broken doll, murdered, and all because some damn female journalist had ignored his explicit instructions so that she could get her human interest story...

'Don't make the mistake of thinking that the fact that we've had sex changes anything,' he told Suzy brutally. 'It doesn't! After all, we both know that sex is the currency you favour. On this occasion it didn't work!'

A cold feeling of sickness was crawling through her. Shock, anguish, despair—she could feel them all.

Luke was making it humiliatingly plain that he had simply used her for sex. How could she have been so stupid as to allow herself to think— To think what? That because for her sexual intimacy was inextricably linked to emotional intimacy Luke would think the same thing? That because she could not stop herself from feeling the way she did about him he shared those feelings? Was she totally crazy? Hadn't he just made it brutally plain to her that he did not?

Silently Suzy turned away from him, whilst pain raked her with burning claws.

CHAPTER EIGHT

'I'M BORED!'

Charlie's petulant comment was a welcome interruption to Suzy's agonised inner examination of what had happened with Luke last night.

She and the children had breakfasted alone, Lucy informing her with a world-weary sigh that, 'Daddy and Luke are talking business and we aren't allowed to interrupt them.'

Was it business that had been responsible for Luke's absence from both the bed they had shared last night and the suite when she had woken up this morning? Suzy didn't really care! She was glad he seemed to have forgotten his threat to stay with her day and night, and was just relieved that she hadn't had to go through the embarrassment and humiliation of seeing him.

In fact she wished passionately that she might never have to see him again! How could he have used her so cold-bloodedly— and more importantly, how could she have let him?

'It's a beautiful day,' she responded to Charlie's statement of his boredom. 'Why don't you go for a swim?'

She had seen the swimming pool from her vantage point on the hillside above the villa, and had admired the elegance of its tranquil setting.

'We can't go swimming,' Charlie told her crossly.

Suzy frowned, wondering if perhaps their father had put a ban on them swimming without adult supervision. But before she could say anything Lucy told her unhappily, 'We can't swim because Mummy sent us with the wrong clothes. She forgot about packing our swimming things.'

Forgot? Suzy felt a sharp stab of anger against the children's mother as she looked at Lucy's downbent head, and wondered cynically if it *was* just that the children's swimming things had been forgotten or if she had deliberately sent them away with the wrong clothes in order to make life difficult for their father.

'Well, perhaps you could ask Daddy to buy some new things for you?' she suggested practically. The resort had any number of shops selling clothes and, whilst they might be expensive, Sir Peter Verey did not strike her as a man who had to watch his budget!

A maid came in to clear away the breakfast things, and through the open door Suzy could see a powerfully built man standing in the hallway.

One of Luke's men? Although there was no obvious evidence of the villa being heavily guarded, Suzy suspected that if she tried to make any attempt to leave she would find that she wasn't allowed to get very far.

Idly she wondered just what it was that demanded Luke's presence here. Certainly the soldiers she had seen departing must have something to do with it. It must be politically delicate rather than dangerous, she suspected, otherwise the children wouldn't be here. Sir Peter might not be a particularly hands-on father, but surely he wouldn't risk exposing his children to danger?

'It's no use us asking Daddy to take us shopping. He'll just say that he's too busy.' Lucy informed Suzy, her words breaking into her thoughts.

The weary resignation in her voice made Suzy's heart ache for her. It told of a small lifetime of being told that her parents were 'too busy'.

'But Suzy could take us! Lucy, let's go and ask Daddy if she can!' Charlie suggested excitedly, getting off his chair.

'If she can what?'

Suzy spun round as Sir Peter and Luke came into the room.

'Daddy, Mummy forgot to pack our swimsuits and our shorts and things,' Lucy answered her father, a little reluctantly.

She obviously felt that what she was saying was a betrayal of her mother, Suzy recognised.

'Yes, and we want Suzy to take us out and buy some new ones,' Charlie added importantly.

Suzy could feel both Sir Peter and Luke looking at her. The relaxed approval in Sir Peter's eyes certainly wasn't mirrored in Luke's.

Suzy's heart gave a painful jerk. The sight of him was releasing the despair and anguish she had been fighting to ignore. Self-contempt and misery crawled through her veins like poison. And yet, as she dragged her gaze from Luke's face, Suzy acknowledged that it wasn't the anger she should be feeling that was making her tremble inwardly, but a destructive and humiliating ache of longing!

She was distantly aware of Sir Peter exclaiming enthusiastically, 'What an excellent idea! My dear, you are a godsend!'

'Peter, I don't think—' Luke began, an ominous expression in his eyes as he cast Suzy a freezing look of contempt.

'Luke, I know you want her all to yourself, and I can't blame you.' Sir Peter smiled. 'But we mustn't disappoint the children!'

Luke had intended to spend the morning catching up on some paperwork and trying to see if there wasn't some way that President Njambla could be pinned down to a definite date in order that he could wind up the whole exercise with as much speed as possible. He told himself he should have guessed that Suzy would try to pull this kind of trick.

He had already given orders that no one was to be allowed to leave the villa without his permission, and thanks to the high wall that surrounded the property it was impossible to leave other than via one of the discreetly guarded gates.

The staff all lived in, and had been thoroughly vetted, and it should have been an easy task to ensure that Suzy did not have any outside contact with anyone. He had taken possession of her mobile phone and her passport.

Taken possession! Luke wished his brain had not supplied him with those two particular words. Last night he had physically taken possession of Suzy herself, but only because his desire for her had taken possession of him!

'Indeed we mustn't,' Luke answered Sir Peter grimly. 'I'll organise a car. Are you ready to leave now?' he asked Suzy curtly.

'Well, I need to go upstairs and get my bag,' Suzy responded shakily as she tried to withstand the look he was giving her.

'I'll come with you,' Luke announced, leaving her with no option other than to walk towards the door, uncomfortably aware as she did so that he was following her.

Halfway up the stairs she asked herself bitterly why, after what he had done to her and what he had said to her, the reaction of her body to the knowledge that he was so close behind her now was one of longing and not rejection.

Quickening her step, she headed for their suite. But as she reached for the door handle

Luke was there before her. Suzy flinched as she felt the brief brush of hard fingertips against her wrist.

'Quite a clever move,' Luke said conversationally as he closed the door, imprisoning her with him in the room's heavy silence. 'I had forgotten that female reporters are different from the rest of their sex and do not possess any scruples where children are concerned.'

There was a look in his eyes that confused Suzy—a mixture of biting contempt and savage anger laced with pain, as though somehow his words had a personal meaning for him.

'I am not using the children!' Suzy denied heatedly. 'It was their idea to approach their father. And besides, I could hardly manufacture the fact that their mother has been spiteful enough to send them here without proper holiday clothes. The dress Lucy was wearing last night looked so uncomfortable. Poor little scraps—I feel so sorry for them,' Suzy told him emotionally.

Luke could feel himself tensing as he listened to her. Why, when he knew she was acting, was he allowing himself to react to her faked emotions, allowing her to needle her way under his professional skin, letting her touch personal nerve-endings he had no damned business allowing her to touch?

'And as for using them! You're a fine one to talk about that!' she accused him angrily. 'You're keeping me imprisoned here because whatever it is that is going on might potentially be dangerous—and yet you are using the children as camouflage!'

'The children's presence here is directly against my wishes,' Luke told her shortly, looking away from her.

'So you mean that there is actually someone who can't be bullied, threatened and coerced into doing what you want?' Suzy couldn't resist demanding.

Immediately Luke turned round, subjecting her to a narrow-eyed gaze that made her want to shiver, as though her flesh had been touched by a blast of cold air.

'Coerced?' Luke challenged her. 'If by that you are trying to imply that last night I coerced you...you certainly didn't give me the impression that you didn't want what was happening. In fact—'

'I don't want to talk about last night,' Suzy interrupted him wildly. 'I don't.'

Was that because she didn't want to have the pathetic remnants of the fantasies and daydreams she was holding onto wrenched from her? Why not? What was the point in stubbornly clinging to them? They were worthless...meaningless...like the physical act she had shared with Luke!

'Save the emotional histrionics for Peter,' Luke told her contemptuously. 'He's becoming besotted enough with you to believe them!'

His words made Suzy frown. Certainly Peter was enjoying pretending to flirt with her, but a pretence at flirtation was all it was. If Suzy could see that she wondered why Luke, who was surely trained to observe and analyse people's behaviour and reactions, could not.

'The children will be waiting,' she told him stiffly. 'I'll just get my bag.'

Before she could move, Luke said, 'Stay here. I'll get it.'

His unexpected chivalrous gesture caught her off guard, but nowhere near so much as his casual question as he picked up a brief-case and opened it.

'Are you all right for money?'

'Yes. I've got enough of my own.' Suzy stopped him quickly.

His concern for her after his earlier comments was like balm on a painful wound, and she watched silently as he closed his case and then crossed the room to pick up her small handbag. It looked tiny grasped in his large hand as he brought it to her.

'And just remember,' he warned her grimly, 'I'm going to be right beside you. If you were thinking—'

'You mean that you're coming with us?'

Luke's hand was pressing against her wrist and Suzy could barely think for the effect his touch was having on her body.

'Why not? You're my partner, after all, and according to Peter I can't bear to let you out of my sight,' he told her derisively.

He certainly wasn't exhibiting any concern for her now, Suzy recognised. He was standing so close that she felt as though she could hardly breathe.

Automatically Suzy stepped back. Her mind and body were tearing her apart with the ferocity of the conflicting messages they were sending her. She wanted to go somewhere quiet and dark and stay there until she felt able to cope. Instead she was going to have to go to the resort, with Luke at her side and a smile pinned to her face.

Impulsively she turned to Luke, driven to get him to believe her and to set her free, but the words died unspoken as she saw the look on his face.

Well, if he could feel contemptuous about her then somehow she would learn to feel the same way about him, she told herself fiercely, and walked towards the door.

As he watched her Luke too was prey to conflicting emotions. He had absolutely no doubt that his suspicions concerning her were correct. And, that being the case, it was essential that he prevented her from having any kind of contact with anyone she might pass information on to. In that sense, in the professional sense, she was his enemy.

But his anger and bitterness towards her because of what she was—they were not professionally objective feelings, in any way, shape or form. They were personal. And on that personal level those feelings were unacceptable, Luke told himself grimly. Unacceptable and potentially prejudicial to his ability to do his job.

When fighting men became battle-weary they ceased to be effective. That was one of the reasons why he had left the Army. Because he had begun to feel he had fought too many wars and seen too much death. Was he now experiencing a similar syndrome within his current work? Was Suzy Roberts getting to him because for some reason he was no longer an effective operative? Or was he no longer an effective operative because Suzy Roberts was getting to him?

It wasn't going to be the latter. No way would he allow himself that weakness! To lose it over a woman like her? To want her, ache for her; hunger for her to the point where those feelings dominated every other aspect of his life?

No way!

Her subtle manipulation of the children this morning proved that he was right to be suspicious of her. So why, knowing all of that, when she had looked at him earlier with that faked pain in her eyes, had he been driven to take her in his arms and—?

And what? And nothing, Luke told himself savagely. Absolutely nothing!

'Luke, there's a parking space.' Suzy called as she looked out of the window of the large four-wheel drive vehicle in which Luke had driven them down to the resort.

'I've seen it,' was Luke's clipped response, and he neatly reversed the large vehicle into the small space.

Her eyes shadowed, Suzy turned her face away from him, angry with herself for letting such a small and unimportant rejection of help bring betraying tears to her eyes. She turned to get out of the Jeep.

'Wait there,' Luke told her imperiously, sliding out of his own seat.

Was he afraid that she might jump out and try to run away? Suzy wondered scathingly as she watched him come round to her own door and open it. Immediately she made to scramble out, but as she did so Luke took hold of her, lifting her bodily out of the car and placing her gently on the ground.

Raw pain scalded Suzy's throat, making it impossible for her to speak as she stood stiffly in his hold.

To anyone looking at them his gesture would have seemed one of loving consideration. But he did not love her. He loathed and despised her!

The pain in her throat had reached her chest. She could feel Luke looking at her, but she refused to return his gaze. She did have some pride, and there was no way she was going to let him see the anguish she knew must be in her eyes.

With a small twist of her body she pulled away from him in mute rejection, and then tensed as she felt him tighten his grip on her, constraining her. Now she *did* look at him, resentment emanating from every pore of her body as she resisted his hold.

What the hell was that damned perfume Suzy was wearing? Luke wondered savagely as the air around filled with the scent of her. It conjured up for him mental images his senses had retained: her body, silky smooth beneath his hands, fire and passion beneath his touch as she moved against him, with him...

A thousand brilliant images flooded his senses as the warm morning air wafted her

scent around him. It might be morning outside his body, but inside it, inside his head,
it was night, with its soft, sensual darkness,
its dangerous memories...

Against his will Luke felt his gaze sliding
slowly from her eyes to her mouth, to absorb
in greedy silence its shape and beauty. His
mouth already knew its texture, her texture,
but those memories were not enough.
Suddenly he wanted to know it again. To
trace its tender outline, to stroke its soft
warmth, to probe the sweet resistance it offered him and capture its innermost sweetness.

Suzy felt as though she was about to collapse. Luke was looking at her mouth and his
look was scorching her, making her want to
lift her face to him and plead for his kiss.
Frantically she dragged her hot gaze away
from his face and looked at the car.

The children! To her shame, she realised
that she had actually forgotten about them!

Her small frantic movement brought Luke
back to reality. Releasing her, he turned towards the car and went to help the children
out.

CHAPTER NINE

'LUKE nearly kissed you then,' Lucy confided innocently to Suzy as she fell into step beside her, whilst her brother, boy-like, immediately stationed himself at Luke's side.

Kissed her? What for? Punishment? A gesture of his contempt? Suzy wondered sadly as the four of them made their way from the car park to the town's quaintly narrow and very steep streets.

'I think there's a children's shop not far from here,' Suzy announced, indicating the small square they were just entering.

Before they had left Sir Peter had handed her a very large sum of euros, telling her to get whatever she thought the children might need. And Suzy intended to do just that! It appalled her that their mother should be so selfish as to send them on holiday without the necessary clothes purely to spite her ex-husband, without giving a thought to how the children themselves might feel.

However, she was by nature thrifty—she had had to be, she acknowledged wryly. So she would get the best she could for the money.

Several cafés fronted onto the ancient cobbled square, their canvas sun umbrellas adding a bright splash of colour to the greyness of the weathered stone.

'It's just down here,' Suzy told Luke, indicating the narrow alleyway in front of them.

The children's clothes shop was three doors down, and Suzy could see Lucy's eyes light up as they walked inside. Within seconds the little girl was standing in silence, absorbed in the racks of clothes. Silent maybe, but her expression said it all, Suzy reflected as she watched the pleasure and excitement illuminating her face.

'Tell me what you think you would like, Lucy,' she suggested. 'And then we can have a look.'

She could feel Luke standing behind her, and in any other circumstances she would have suggested that he take Charlie to the other side of the shop and pick out some clothes for him. But she was too conscious of Luke's biting statement that he was going to remain glued to her side to do so.

Instead she waited patiently whilst Lucy went slowly through the rack, stopping every now and then to look enquiringly at Suzy.

'You need a couple of swimsuits and some shorts, Lucy,' Suzy said gently. 'Some tee shirts, and perhaps a dress?'

A tender smile curled her mouth as she saw that Lucy was hovering over a trendy pre-teen outfit of which wasn't really suitable for holidaywear, but Suzy could see its appeal for her.

Watching the interplay between child and woman, Luke reminded himself angrily that Suzy was a skilled actress.

More than an hour after they had entered the shop both children were kitted out, and

Lucy's face was glowing with delight because Suzy had ruefully agreed that she could have the outfit she had set her heart on.

'Can we have an ice cream now?' Charlie asked as soon as they reached the square.

'It's almost lunchtime,' Luke told him, but instead of insisting that they needed to return to the villa to Suzy's surprise he suggested that they find a table at one of the cafés and have an early lunch there.

'Yes!' Charlie exclaimed excitedly.

Five minutes later they were sitting at a table, menus in their hands.

'Suzy, do you think I could wear my new trousers for dinner tonight?' Lucy asked earnestly, after the waiter had taken their order.

Suzy couldn't help it. Over Lucy's head her gaze met Luke's, her eyes brimming with tender amusement.

'I don't see why not—so long as your father doesn't mind,' she agreed.

Completely happy, Lucy leaned her head against Suzy and stroked her bare arm with loving fingers.

Her small, innocent gesture and the message of trust it carried made Luke feel as though a giant clamp was tightening around his heart.

How could one woman be two such very different people?

Different? What the hell was he thinking? She was only one person—a devious, manipulative, despicable person, incapable of any kind of genuine emotion.

The waiter brought their food, and Suzy was just beginning to eat hers when she happened to glance across the square.

Shock froze her into immobility as she saw the man standing only yards away and immediately recognised him. Jerry Needham! He was one of the reporters from the magazine; one of the men who had made her life such a misery when she had worked there.

What was he doing here? Taking a holiday? Or something more sinister—like trying to find out what was going on at the villa? Her heart was jerking around inside her chest as though someone had it on a string. What if he saw her and came over? Introduced himself? Luke would immediately suspect the worst.

Her appetite had completely deserted her, but then she saw Jerry was walking away from them and disappearing into the crowd on the other side of the square. Suzy tried to relax, but her insides were a tight ball of anxiety and apprehension. She had never liked Jerry—he was loud-mouthed, boorish and vulgar, and the sexual innuendo of the comments he had made to her had filled her with nausea. But she knew that he was an exceptionally shrewd reporter.

To her relief she heard Luke asking the children, 'Finished, you two?' He signalled for the waiter and asked Suzy, 'If you're ready to go…?'

Suzy was on her feet before he had finished speaking, but they had no sooner walked back into the crowded square when Charlie suddenly piped up urgently. 'I need the bathroom!'

An innocent enough request, but it was one that caused the two adults who heard it to tense in silent dismay.

One look at Charlie's screwed-up and anxious face told Suzy that there was no way the little boy could wait.

'There must have been lavatories back at the café,' she told Luke. 'You'll have to take him back there. Lucy and I will wait here.'

Luke looked down at Charlie and inwardly cursed. The square was busy and Charlie was only young—there was no way he could let him go alone. It was obvious that he would have to take him to the lavatory. Which meant that he would have to leave Suzy here unguarded.

'Why don't you take Lucy?' he suggested, as Charlie tugged anxiously on his arm.

'I don't want to go.' Lucy forestalled his attempt to at least keep some check on Suzy.

'We'll wait here for you,' Suzy told him, quickly checking the crowd to make sure there was no sign of the reporter.

Luke hurried Charlie through the crowd. He could not blame the little boy for what had happened, and neither could he accuse Suzy of having engineered the situation.

How much longer were Luke and Charlie going to be? Suzy wondered anxiously, willing them to return so that they could leave.

'Lucy, where are you going?' she protested as Lucy suddenly started to hurry towards one of the stalls.

'It's all right, I just want to look at something,' Lucy called back to her.

Suzy suddenly froze as the crowd parted and a couple of yards behind her she saw Jerry—looking right back at her.

She turned away, hoping to disappear into the throng of sightseers, but he was too quick for her, and she tensed as she felt his hand on her arm.

'Suzy! Suzy Roberts! What a coincidence!'

The oily, speculative look he was giving her made Suzy feel sick as it brought back unwanted memories.

'What are you doing here?' he demanded, still watching her with a look in his eyes which Suzy did not like.

'I'm on holiday with my partner,' Suzy lied uncomfortably, adding quickly, 'I must go. He'll be wondering where I am—we got separated by the crowd.' Turning away from him, she went to where Lucy was standing, looking at a stall selling handmade jewellery.

'Why didn't you stay where I left you?'

Suzy could hear the censorious note in Luke's voice. Had he seen Jerry? She looked round anxiously, but the reporter was nowhere to be seen.

'I wanted to look at one of the stalls,' Lucy answered sunnily. 'Are we going back to the villa now?'

'Yes, we are,' Luke agreed.

Suzy shivered as she saw him looking searchingly at her. Surely if he had seen Jerry with her he would have said something, only too delighted to have his suspicions of her confirmed? But it was not so much her fear that Luke might have seen Jerry with her that was making her feel so anxious, Suzy acknowledged as Luke guided them through the crowd, it was her concern about the reporter's presence here in the resort, so close to the villa.

The owner of the magazine did have excellent sources of sensitive information, although who they were Suzy had never known. It was not entirely beyond the bounds of possibility that Roy Jarvis could have sent Jerry to Italy to check up on what was happening at the villa.

And, that being the case, didn't she, as an honest citizen, have a moral obligation to tell Luke that she had seen him?

From his vantage point several yards away Jerry watched Luke and Suzy making their way through the crowd with the two children.

He had recognised Luke, of course, and unless he was mistaken—and he was sure that he was not—those two kids with them were the Verey kids, who were staying with their father.

Jerry had only arrived at the resort the previous day, sent there to check out a tip-off about Sir Peter Verey's real reason for being in Italy. Now he had the happy feeling that things were very definitely going his way!

Suzy Roberts and Lucas Soames. Well, well, what a piece of luck!

Suzy was still struggling with her moral dilemma when they got back to the villa.

Jerry might just be at the resort on holiday, or even following some other story involving the celebrities who stayed there, she tried to tell herself. But her conscience refused to be convinced.

CHAPTER TEN

'LUKE, can I have a word?'

Luke frowned as the operative he had put in charge of the perimeter security at the villa approached him.

It was twenty-four hours since he had driven Suzy and the children back from the resort—twenty-four hours, far too many of which he had spent fighting against his own emotions instead of concentrating on his professional business, which was why he had this morning finally instructed one of his London operatives to supply him with a full and detailed report on Suzy. He was sure the information in the report would back up his professional distrust of her and help him to banish these unwanted emotions she was causing him! The more information he had about her, the better.

Last night after dinner he had escorted Suzy to their suite and pretended to busy himself with some work whilst she prepared for bed. Only when he had been sure she was soundly asleep had he gone to bed himself, and even then he had not been able to relax.

In her sleep she had turned over to lie facing him, and he had wanted...

Luke did not want to think about what he had wanted to do.

Unable to trust himself not to give in to the temptation she represented, he had got up and spent the rest of the night sleeping uncomfortably in a chair.

He had got up and dressed before she had woken, though, determined not to allow her to suspect how vulnerable he had become to her. He had even caught himself thinking that if things could be different, if they could somehow find a way... To what? he had challenged himself. To forget what she was and what she did? Impossible! Furiously angry with himself, he wished he had never set eyes on her.

She was with the Verey children now, sun-bathing beside the pool. The swimsuit she had been wearing when he had walked past earlier had made him remember what it had felt like to hold her naked body.

Hell, but he would be glad when all this was over.

'Yes, Phillips, what is it?' he asked his operative.

'The guards have reported that a chap's been hanging around the gates, asking questions about Ms Roberts.'

Luke's eyes narrowed. 'What chap?' he demanded grimly.

Hugh Phillips was young and keen, and quickly told Luke what he knew.

'He said he was just a friend, and refused to give any name, but according to the guards he was asking rather too many questions—and not just about Ms Roberts.'

Luke felt his stomach churn with anger—and something else! What the hell was he feeling like *that* for? He ought to be feeling vindicated, because he had been right to suspect Suzy, instead of savagely angry.

'Well, if he's so keen to see Ms Roberts, then perhaps he should be allowed to do so, Hugh. Tell the guards to allow him to persuade them to let him in. Don't make it too easy for him, though. I don't want him getting suspicious. We need to know who he is and what he's up to. Keep him away from the house. You can let Ms Roberts meet him in the surrounds.'

Luke could see that Hugh Phillips was battling not to show any reaction to the mention of Suzy's name. Like everyone else, Hugh believed that Suzy was Luke's own partner.

'Have you got all that?' he checked coolly.

'Yes,' Hugh answered woodenly.

'Good—and remember, the minute he comes back I want to know!'

Once Hugh had gone Luke went to stand in front of the window of the small room he used as his office.

He had received unofficial confirmation this morning that the African President was

finally satisfied with the security arrangements and was prepared to set a firm date for
the meeting.

With that in view, and his suspicions re-
garding Suzy confirmed, he should be feeling
pleased. Instead of which he felt strangely
disappointed. Suzy must somehow have
made contact with her 'friend' when he had
had to take Charlie to the lavatory, and that
was surely a predictable move on her part, so
why was he feeling as though what she had
done was some kind of personal betrayal?
What the hell was happening to him? He was
thinking—feeling—more like a betrayed
lover than a man with no emotional involve-
ment with her.

And as for the man who had come asking
for her! Her 'friend'… Luke's muscles
clenched against the pain of the surge of jealousy and male anger that pounded through
him. He had to be someone from the magazine—not Roy Jarvis, of course. Another reporter, perhaps.

They would soon know, Luke promised himself, and when Suzy did meet up with him he would need to know what was being said.

He unlocked one of the drawers in his desk and searched through until he had found what he wanted. The minute recording device lying on the palm of his hand was so sophisticated that it was almost impossible to believe that so much technology could be packed into such a small thing. Designed to be slipped underneath a watch, it could record and transmit conversations with remarkable clarity. It could also reveal the location of the wearer to within a metre.

Slipping it on his own watch, Luke locked the drawer and left the room...

'Look, Suzy, watch me dive!' Charlie shouted as he jumped into the swimming pool, sending up a splash of water.

'That isn't a dive,' Lucy told him scornfully when he got out. 'You just jumped in.'

'Yes, it was. It was a dive,' Charlie argued.

'No, it wasn't—was it, Suzy?' Lucy appealed.

'Yes, it was,' Charlie continued to insist.

Ruefully Suzy got up and went over to them. She had a bit of a headache—a legacy from not being able to sleep properly last night, she suspected.

She had gone to bed before Luke, all too relieved to be able to shower and quickly jump into bed whilst he was still in the suite's sitting room. But, much as she had longed to fall asleep before he joined her in the large bed, her guilty conscience had refused to let her.

Eventually she had dropped off, only to wake up to discover that she had turned over and was now lying facing Luke, one hand outstretched, as though she was trying to reach out to him in her sleep. Afraid of waking him up if she moved, she had lain there motionless, worrying about Jerry and what he was doing so close to the villa.

She had still been awake when Luke had suddenly slid out of the bed to pad naked into the suite's sitting room.

The large bed had felt empty and lonely without him, and she had found herself moving over to where he had been lying so that she could breathe in the scent of him from the warm sheets and pillows.

He had been up and dressed when she had woken this morning, and she had been under no illusion as to why he had waited in the sitting room for her whilst she showered and dressed.

In grim silence he had accompanied her downstairs for breakfast, and then later out here, to the swimming pool.

And she still hadn't told him about Jerry! Because there hadn't been any opportunity to do so, she tried to reassure herself.

'Luke's here.'

Lucy's pleased announcement broke into her thoughts and brought a swift surge of colour to her skin.

Hoping that he wouldn't see it, and guess at its cause, Suzy pretended not to have heard Lucy's statement and kept her head down, moving only when Charlie suddenly jumped into the pool and she was showered with water.

'See—that isn't a dive, it's a jump,' Lucy pronounced as Suzy shook the water off her face and stood up. 'Tell him, Luke,' she begged. 'Tell him that he can't dive.'

Smiling at the little girl, Luke surveyed the protected area around the pool. Suzy had left her wrap by her lounger, and when Luke turned his head to look at her an intensely strong physical reaction kicked at her stomach. She could feel her nipples peaking and thrusting provocatively against the fabric of her swimsuit, and she knew from the downward sweep of Luke's eyelashes that he was looking at their wanton flaunting.

She took a deep breath and fought off the desire to wrap her arms tightly around her body.

Luke cursed himself under his breath as he fought to drag his gaze away from Suzy's body. Already the evidence of her swollen nipples was affecting him—arousing him. All it would take was one step forward and then he could tug those thin swimsuit straps down her shoulders and expose the full creaminess of her breasts to his hands and his lips. He could take each of those nipples into his mouth in turn and show them what they were inciting when they tormented his senses until his self-control was at breaking point.

'Luke, Luke—tell her that I can dive.'

Charlie's high-pitched voice broke through the heated pressure of his thoughts, and quickly he turned away from Suzy. Her watch was lying on a small table, along with her sunglasses and some suntan cream. Luke walked towards it.

'Watch this, then!'

There was the sound of a noisy splash, followed almost immediately by an angry scream. Suzy swung round to see Lucy standing beside the pool, dripping wet from Charlie's 'dive'.

His small task completed, Luke strolled over to help calm the commotion.

From now on, until he removed the small device, every sound Suzy made, even down to her heartbeat, would be transmitted to the receiver locked in his desk. There wouldn't be a single word she spoke, a single breath she took whilst she was with her 'friend' that he would not know about!

As she towelled Charlie dry Suzy looked over his head to where Luke was standing. She could tell him now, her conscience prodded her. All she needed to do was open her mouth and just say the words.

But what if he doesn't believe me? What if he thinks that I'm lying, that I'm part of whatever it is that's going on?

What if he did? her conscience demanded sternly. Were her own personal feelings really more important than something that was obviously very serious?

Suzy took a deep breath.

'Luke?'

She stopped speaking when his mobile started to ring, and watched in heavy-hearted disappointment as he answered it and began to walk away.

She could always tell him later, she comforted herself as she reached for her wrap and informed the children it was time to go inside. Perhaps this evening, whilst they were alone and getting ready for dinner.

Her heart did a back somersault that caused just as much devastation inside her chest as Charlie's 'dives' had done around the pool!

'He's back—refuses to give any name, but he's biting on the bait we've floated. He's offered the two guards a fistful of euros to let him in. The guards are making sure he has to work hard to persuade them, and I've told them to say they'll let him in through that side gate in the perimeter wall.'

'The one closest to the lake and the grotto?' Luke questioned sharply.

'Yes, that's the one—is that okay?'

'Yes, that's fine. What's he going to do when he gets in, though? I don't want him wandering freely anywhere.'

'That's okay. Nico is going to ask him if he wants a message sent to Ms Roberts, arranging to meet her.'

'Okay, let me know when he's taken the bait, Hugh.'

Suzy had just showered and changed when she heard a knock on the door of the suite.

Going to open it, she was surprised to see a young Italian standing there.

'I have a message for you, miss,' he announced, before Suzy could speak. 'There is a man—a friend of yours. He wishes you to meet him beside the grotto.'

Suzy stared at him, her heart hammering with apprehension.

'What man? Who is this man?' she began to demand, but the Italian was already walking quickly away from her.

It was Jerry—it had to be. Although how on earth he had got into the grounds and past Luke's guards Suzy could not imagine.

Anxiously she rushed down the stairs and out into the garden, glancing at her watch as she did so. The lake and the grotto were quite a long walk away from the villa, and she kept looking anxiously around herself as she hurried towards them.

She skirted the lake using the footpath, hurrying past the sign that warned against anyone entering the grotto because it was unsafe. A padlocked iron gate guarded the entrance, and Suzy frowned to see that there was a key in the lock. She must mention it at the villa, just in case the children should stray down this way!

Once she reached the other side of the grotto she paused, looking around uncertainly and then tensing when Jerry suddenly stepped out of the shadow of the trees and shrubs where he had been waiting for her.

'Jerry! What are you doing? How did you get in here?' she demanded apprehensively.

'Never mind that.' He stopped her curtly. 'I want to know what's going on here. Come on, Suzy, spill the beans. What a piece of luck, finding you here. We got a tip-off that there was something important going on.'

'There's nothing going on,' Suzy lied determinedly. Jerry's comments had confirmed her worst fears. She was certainly not going to tell him anything! But perhaps if she found out what Jerry was up to the information might actually be useful to Luke—as well as help to prove her own innocence.

'Oh, come off it! If that's true what's Soames doing here? And how did you get hooked up with him anyway?'

'We're here on holiday, that's all—and as to how Luke and I met, that's not really any of your business,' Suzy told him coolly.

In his office Luke frowned as he listened in on their conversation. Had Suzy somehow realised that they were on to her?

'"Luke and I"?' Jerry mimicked sneeringly. 'Typical that you'd go for someone like Soames—he's as bloody moralistic as you are! Met those kids of his yet, have you?'

Suzy's heart somersaulted. Kids? Luke had children? And children meant a mother, a woman he loved. No, that couldn't be true.

'Just as well he's wealthy. I've heard that their medical bills will run into thousands. Risking his own life to save some refugee brats! I'd have left 'em, myself. Got shot for his pains, didn't he?'

Refugee brats? As she rcoiled from Jerry's unpleasantness Suzy felt the tight band of pain around her heart slacken a little. There was no woman Luke loved enough to give her his children. But this was no time to think about her own feelings.

'You've got to leave, Jerry,' she insisted shakily. 'There's nothing happening here of any interest to you or the magazine.'

'You're lying,' Jerry accused her, putting his face so close to Suzy's that she stepped back. 'The boss has had a tip-off. That's why I'm here. Knew I'd got lucky when I saw you with the Verey kids.'

'They're here on holiday with their father.'

'They may be on holiday, but Verey's here for something more than that—and that's why Soames is here as well. They've got guards on the gate, for goodness' sake.'

'The owner of the villa employs the guards,' Suzy fibbed inventively. 'And, as I have just told you, Luke and I are here on holiday. Sir Peter is a friend of Luke's and he invited us to stay.'

'Sleeping with Soames, are you?'

Luke heard the small indrawn breath Suzy took before she told him firmly, 'Yes, of course I am.'

'Well, that's turn-up, isn't it? Little Miss Don't-Touch-Me-I'm-Only-Just-This-Side-of-Being-a-Virgin crawling into bed with Soames. The boss wasn't too pleased with you for leaving like that, you know. He'd got a pretty heavy bet set up that he'd be the one to teach you a thing or two about sex.'

Jerry was leering at her and Suzy had to fight down her furious disgust.

'Good, is he? Soames? I reckon you owe the boss one for depriving him of his pleasure. Come on, Suzy, tell me what's going on—for old times' sake.'

Suzy had had enough.

'For old times' sake?' she snapped, her eyes flashing with fury. 'You and the rest of those disgusting men at the magazine made my life a misery. And if you think for one moment that if there was anything to tell—which there isn't—I would betray national secrets to someone like you... Well, if you want my advice, Jerry, you should leave here right now—before—'

'Before what?' Jerry stopped her, an ugly look on his face. 'Before you go running to Luke to give the game away?'

A chilly little breeze seemed to have sprung up, and Suzy shivered. Suddenly she felt not just cold but frightened as well.

'Jerry, I don't know what you want,' she began, but Jerry stopped her.

'You know damned well what I want,' he told her viciously. 'I want to know what's going on here, and one way or another I intend to find out.'

As he spoke he reached out and grabbed Suzy's arm, looking past her at the grotto.

'Jerry—what are you doing? Jerry, let me go!' Suzy started to protest, trying to resist as he dragged her towards the grotto and unlocked the iron gate.

'Let's see if you feel a bit more like talking after a few hours in here,' he told Suzy, panting heavily as he released her and gave her a savage push.

Suzy cried out as she lost her balance.

'Jerry, it isn't safe in here,' she protested anxiously as she struggled to get to her feet. But Jerry wasn't listening to her. Instead he was locking her inside the grotto and walking away with the key.

Luke cursed as he got to his feet, rapping out a message to Hugh Phillips to apprehend Jerry. Giving a cursory glance through the office window, he started to hurry out of the villa.

He had been wrong about Suzy! Utterly and completely wrong. And beneath his surprise at the discovery, and his concern for the danger she was in, he could feel a swift, deep tide of joy running through him.

Locked in the grotto, Suzy tried not to give in to her fear. Someone was bound to come past and rescue her, surely? One of the gardeners, or one of Luke's men.

She tensed as she heard a low, threatening rumble. Stones and debris were falling all around her. Panicking, she ran to the back of the grotto, to avoid being hit by the growing avalanche of boulders, and then gave a terrified scream as the ground suddenly gave way beneath her.

She was falling down some kind of tunnel, Suzy recognised, with twigs and soil raining down all around her in the darkness. And then suddenly her fall came to an end, and the air jolted out of her lungs as she hit the cold dampness of a hard earth floor.

Somewhere in the distance she could still hear rumbling, but as she strained her ears to listen to it abruptly it ceased and there was silence.

Silence and darkness.

Her body hurt, but her fear was much greater than her physical pain. She was trapped somewhere underground beneath the grotto. Dust filled the air above and around her, making her cough and gag. How long would it be before someone found her—if they found her at all?

CHAPTER ELEVEN

LUKE had once run for his school—and, alerted by the sound of falling rocks, he reached the grotto just as it started to collapse in on itself. White-faced he looked at the pile of rubble beneath which Suzy was now buried.

Whilst his mind was coolly and mechanically planning what had to be done his heart was racing, thudding, swelling with emotions he couldn't afford to allow to torment him.

'Get on to the emergency services!' he shouted over his shoulder to Hugh, who had followed him. 'And then get the men down here!'

Suzy! Anguish, guilt, despair—he could feel all of them. Why had he waited so long? Why hadn't he come for her the moment he had realised she had not lied to him? Why had he allowed her to be placed in danger in the first place?

Suzy, Suzy, Suzy. He could feel her name ringing inside his head, inside his heart.

The guards had arrived and quickly he began to instruct them, telling them what to do as he began to move heavy boulders.

As he worked, grimly Luke tried to blot out images of another place and another time. Another pile of debris oozing dust and silence. That one under the heat of the sun, with the taste of smoke and anger in his mouth, the shocked wailing of the bereaved rising from the throats of women as he had looked in bitter fury at the house so unnecessarily destroyed, people killed and maimed by their own. A young woman dead, her children buried beneath the rubble of their home.

'Luke, if they are in there they'll be dead,' one of his comrades had muttered to him, but Luke had ignored him.

They had found the baby first, perfectly still, and then the older child. Luke knew he hadn't been the only one who had wept.

Those images were inside his head now, those images and those desperate feelings. He had hurt then, for those children, but if he had feared for them then that was nothing to what he was feeling right now.

And, what was more, Luke knew that it would not have made one iota of difference to him right now if Suzy *had* been colluding with the magazine, if she *had* been about to betray a hundred security secrets—he loved her, and his love for her was the strongest and most powerful emotion he had ever felt. It was so strong, in fact, that he had been afraid of it—afraid of acknowledging its power over him, afraid of admitting it to himself.

Suzy! He had loved her, he suspected, from the minute he had felt the brush of her soft lips against his own.

'Luke! Take it easy!'

It was only when he felt Hugh's restraining hand on his arm that he realised that he was tearing at the fallen boulders, his throat blocked with the pain of crying her name.

* * *

They worked late into the evening, under searchlights which had been rigged up and with the teams of experts Luke had called in.

Several times Luke was told to take a break and allow others to continue with the task that their expertise equipped them for, but he refused to listen. What he wouldn't give for a team of trained sappers here right now, he thought bitterly, as he watched the painfully slow progress, grim-faced.

If Suzy died it would be his fault. He would have killed her, killed the woman he loved, the woman he should have cherished and protected above everyone and anyone else, even above and beyond his duty. That was how he felt about her. How he would always feel about her. Admitting his love for her had been like taking a bung out of a dyke. The pressure of his denied feelings was pouring through him, drowning out everything else.

Why hadn't he listened to his emotions? Why had he persisted in disbelieving her and them?

He knew the answer to that, Luke acknowledged, his gaze never wavering from the harsh beam of light directed on to the fallen rocks. He had been afraid of admitting the truth.

He had decided a long time ago not to marry. He had seen too many Army marriages fall apart under the strain it imposed on them and he had thought he could prevent himself from falling in love, from wanting to spend the rest of his life with that one special person. Until Suzy had come into his life.

Into his life! And out of it?

The harsh lights bleached the colour from his face, leaving it leached of blood, his eyes two dark, burning sockets of pain fixed on the spot beneath which Suzy lay.

For Suzy, trapped inside her small cave, time blurred.

She was a child again, trying to comfort her crying mother, telling her everything would be all right—only her mother wasn't there, and she was the one who was crying.

Images and memories came and went, sweeping over her in waves of semi-consciousness. Curled up in a foetal position, she relived the happiest of her memories and experiences. And thought of Luke, whose name, whose taste would surely be on her lips as she took her last breath...

Luke stood grim-lipped in front of the Italian in charge of the rescue operation.

'I do not care how well trained your men are,' he told him curtly. 'I go in first. And now.'

It was nearly midnight, and the rescue team had managed to tunnel down to where Suzy was trapped—thanks, in the main, to Luke's experience and leadership. The watch Suzy was wearing had registered the fact that she was still breathing, and the bugging device had also helped them pinpoint her location. They had discovered that Suzy had fallen down some kind of tunnel or shaft, and now lay in a small space below it.

'It is still too risky for anyone to go in!' the Italian protested, trying to sound authoritative but failing when confronted by Luke's implacable will and air of command. He tried to persist. 'It will be several more hours before we can send someone in to bring out the young lady.'

'I'm going in now,' Luke told him bluntly.

'The tunnel is not yet secure. It could collapse and bury you both,' he warned, but Luke wasn't listening to him. He had already gathered together everything he might need, including medical equipment, food and water.

As the leader of the rescuers had said, the newly dug tunnel still wasn't safe. Its roof needed strengthening before they could risk bringing Suzy out. But it was strong enough to allow Luke to go to her, and that was exactly what he intended to do. No matter what the risk to himself. He had to be with her!

Moving carefully, Luke crawled slowly through the tunnel. He had never liked tunnelling, it made him feel slightly claustro-

phobic and all too aware of his own vulner-
ability, but right now he wouldn't have cared
how long the tunnel was just so long as it
took him to Suzy.

The brightness of the torch Luke was carrying woke Suzy from the exhausted doze she
had fallen into.

Confused, and half in shock, she thought
for a moment that she was hallucinating
when she saw Luke crawling into the small
space illuminated by the torch.

'Luke!' Her voice shook, and so did her
body. 'Luke!' she repeated. 'How…?
What…?'

Her words were smothered against his
chest as he took her in his arms and held her
there—held her as though he was never going
to let her go, Suzy thought. She made a
sound. Something between a laugh and a
whimper, shivering as she clung to the
warmth of his body.

'It's so cold in here, and so dark. I
thought…' She fell silent, unable to tell him

that she had feared she would die here, in this small dark space beneath the ground. 'Are we going to get out now?' she asked him looking towards the tunnel.

'Soon,' Luke answered, giving their surroundings one searching inspection and then switching off the torch—partially to save its light for when they needed it, but also to save Suzy the reality of seeing how dangerous their prison was.

The feel of her in his arms was making his heart thud heavily with emotion. He was with her. He was holding her safe, as he should have held her all along. His hand cupped her face and stroked her hair whilst his other arm held her close to his body.

Half dazed, Suzy decided that she must be imagining the soft brush of Luke's lips against her hair, that it was a fantasy she was allowing herself to drift into.

Even so, she reached out a dusty hand to touch him. Something about the darkness and their intimacy was allowing her to drop the barriers she had put up against him to protect herself.

'I'm so glad you're here. I was afraid I was going to die here.'

Something about the quality of his silence made her tremble.

'We are going to get out of here, aren't we, Luke?' They must be—otherwise he wouldn't be here with her, risking his own life.

There was just the merest pause, the merest missed rhythm in his heartbeat before he told her calmly, 'Yes, of course we are. But we could be here for a while yet.'

'A while?' Suzy's own heart started to thump. 'But if it isn't safe what—? Why—?' Her mouth had gone dry.

'I owe you an apology, Suzy,' Luke told her lightly. 'And now that I've got you to myself, I have got the perfect opportunity to deliver it.'

He was trying to make light of the situation, Suzy recognised, her heart flooding with bittersweet emotion.

There was so much Luke wanted to say to her, but he was fully aware that up above them every sound from their chamber was being monitored via Suzy's watch—hardly an asset when one wanted to whisper words of love and regret.

As he touched her wrist Suzy opened her mouth to ask what he was doing, but Luke silenced her, placing his finger against her lips as he removed the small device and muffled it.

'What—?' Suzy demanded when he'd finished.

'It's what's commonly referred to as a "bug",' Luke told her wryly.

'You *bugged* me?'

The pain in her voice tore at his heart.

'I had no choice,' he told her quietly. He gave a small sigh. 'I do owe you an apology, Suzy—we both know that.'

'You were just doing your job.'

Her defence of him made him wonder grimly how he could ever have thought of doubting her. Her honesty was so patently obvious.

'How long are we going to be down here, Luke?'

'I don't know,' he admitted honestly. 'Are you feeling okay? I've brought some water, and they will be putting an airline through the tunnel.'

'An airline?' Suzy's body trembled. 'You mean in case the tunnel collapses again?'

That was exactly what Luke did mean, and he cursed himself inwardly for adding to her distress.

'It's just a precaution,' he tried to reassure her.

Suzy felt faint and sick. Even with Luke so close to her, holding her, she still felt afraid, her thoughts going round and round.

'We could die in here,' she said in a small panicky voice.

'Don't think about it,' Luke advised her firmly.

'Talk to me, Luke,' Suzy begged him, desperate to have her mind taken off their danger.

'What do you want me to talk to you about?' Luke responded.

'Tell me about the children you rescued,' she replied.

Half of her still didn't dare to believe that he was actually here with her, that she wasn't alone any more. She needed to hear his voice to keep her fears at bay.

Sensing what she was feeling, Luke hesitated and then settled her more comfortably against his body, frowning a little as he realised how cold she was.

The children! Those were the very last memories he wanted to resurrect right now, but how could he deny Suzy anything?

'What do you want to know about them?' he asked quietly.

'Everything,' Suzy answered. 'But first tell me—are they all right now?'

'They're recovering,' Luke told her slowly, 'and with time, and proper medical care, hopefully they will be able to return and live reasonably normal lives. Raschid, the little boy, lost an arm.'

He felt Suzy's tension and cursed himself beneath his breath for having told her.

'Halek, the little girl—the baby—is fine,' he added.

'And their parents—their mother?' Suzy asked tentatively, not really sure why she felt so impelled to ask that particular question.

Was she reading his mind? Luke wondered helplessly.

'Both dead.'

'Tell me what happened,' Suzy whispered.

She could feel the rise and fall of Luke's chest as he breathed in and then exhaled slowly.

'The children's mother was helping us with information. Her husband, their father, had been killed trying to resist the tyranny they were facing. She wanted to avenge his death by helping us to set her people free. It was a dangerous situation for her, and important that we kept her identity hidden, that no one gave away the fact that she was helping us.'

'But someone did,' Suzy hazarded, lifting her head from its resting place against Luke's shoulder to try to peer up into his face.

'Yes,' he agreed heavily. 'Someone did.'

She could feel his remembered anger in the increased thud of his heartbeat, and suddenly out of nowhere she knew!

'Was it—was she a reporter?' she guessed intuitively.

She was still looking up at him; he could tell by her her gentle breaths as they fell on his face.

'Yes, she was,' he confirmed. 'Somehow or other she'd heard about Maram and decided to she wanted to interview her for a human interest story. Of course I informed her that she was going to do no such thing, and I pointed out to her the danger she would be putting Maram in. She ignored my warning, though, and managed to find a young rookie soldier foolish enough to be seduced by her—and I mean literally—into giving her Maram's name. Two days after she interviewed her Maram was murdered, and that was when I found out what Sarah had done.'

'Perhaps she didn't realise the danger she was exposing her to,' Suzy suggested huskily.

'Oh, she realised all right,' Luke told Suzy harshly. 'I had told her myself. But she just didn't care. Nothing mattered more to her than getting her story—not even another woman's life. She even had the gall to try to photograph Maram's children as they were being lifted out of the rubble of their home— the rubble that still contained their mother's body!'

'Jerry said that you have taken financial responsibility for the children,' Suzy murmured.

'They needed medical attention they couldn't get in their own country, and they could only be brought to the UK for treatment if someone agreed to sponsor them. It was the least I could do, seeing as I was responsible for the death of their mother.'

'No! It wasn't your fault,' Suzy protested immediately.

'I was the Commanding Officer, and I'd had enough experience of the determination of reporters to get their story to realise that this particular reporter wasn't going to put another woman's life before her own career,' Luke responded grimly.

'And is that why you hate women reporters?' Suzy asked him quietly. 'Because of what she did?'

'Well, let's just say that she reinforced everything I'd already experienced and felt about them as a breed,' Luke acknowledged. 'One woman murdered, two children nearly killed, three of my men shot and a gunshot wound myself didn't exactly endear her type to me!'

'You were shot?' Suzy exclaimed anxiously, before putting two and two together and asking softly, 'That scar—is that—?'

'Yes,' Luke told her tersely, anticipating her question, before continuing. 'Fortunately the children are survivors—and once they are medically fit to do so they will be returning to their own country to live with their mother's sister, who will love them as her own. Why are you crying?' he asked Suzy gently.

'I'm not,' Suzy fibbed.

But she was, and her tears were tears of sadness for the children and tears of joy for herself, because she was so proud of the man she loved.

The man she loved! Suddenly Suzy wanted to tell him how she felt, how much she loved him. How she had believed the first time she had seen him that fate had brought them together and that he was her one true love, her soul mate. It didn't matter any more that he didn't share her feelings, or that he didn't love her back. She wasn't going to die without saying the words that were locked up inside her heart.

'Luke,' she began shakily, 'if we don't get out of here I—'

'We *will* get out,' Luke began, and then stopped speaking as a sudden rumbling above them had them both looking upwards. 'Don't worry,' he reassured her. 'It just means that they're closer to getting us out, that's all.'

Suzy stared into the darkness, wishing she could see his face and his eyes so that she might have some clue as to what expression they were holding and if he really believed what he was saying or was merely trying to comfort her.

'Suzy—'

The raw urgency of the way Luke was saying her name had Suzy turning to him.

'This is all my fault,' he told her grimly. 'If I hadn't been so determined not to believe you—'

Suzy felt the pad of his thumb brush against her lips.

'I'm sorry, Suzy,' she heard him whisper. 'Oh, God, I am so sorry. I'd give anything, do anything, to get you out of here safely.'

Suzy could feel the warmth of his breath against her mouth, and suddenly, sweetly, she recognised that he was going to kiss her. She was lifting her face towards him when they both heard the sound of activity in the tunnel.

A shower of debris fell down from the ceiling above them, and immediately Luke moved to cover Suzy's body with his own.

'Luke, what's happening?' she demanded, terrified.

'It's all right,' Luke reassured her, holding her tightly. 'Everything's going to be all right. We'll soon be out of here.'

Just hearing his voice made her feel better, Suzy acknowledged as she leaned into him, soaking up the comfort of his presence and his warmth whilst his hand shielded her head from the stones rattling down around them.

Suzy was still wrapped in Luke's arms ten minutes later when their rescuers arrived.

'Take Suzy first,' Luke instructed them. But when they came to lift her away from him she could hardly bear to let go!

CHAPTER TWELVE

'LUKE?'

The moment he heard the small, anxious cry Luke was awake, throwing off the duvet he had covered himself with and padding across the suite to where Suzy was lying frozen with terror in the middle of the large bed.

It was three days since they had been rescued from the grotto, and every night Suzy had had the same nightmare. Every night Luke had gone to her to take her in his arms, to comfort her and reassure her that she was safe. And once he had done that he had gone back to his makeshift bed on one of the sofas.

It was Suzy who had been insistent that there was no point in declaring now that they were not partners—not with the African President's visit so imminent.

'You've got enough to worry about without having to explain who I really am,' she

219

had told Luke when he had told her that although he would prefer it if she didn't leave the villa until after the meeting, he would, if she wanted, make it clear to Sir Peter that they were not partners and ensure that she was provided with her own room.

In the event it was perhaps just as well that they were still sharing the suite. Her nightmare had woken her every night, leaving her shivering with cold and fear, only able to go back to sleep once he was holding her safely in his arms.

'They'll stop soon,' Suzy had told him last night, her teeth chattering as she clung to him.

Luke hadn't said anything. Locked away in his desk drawer was the report he had commissioned on her. And the information it contained had increased his guilt and his shame. She was innocent of everything he had accused her of. She had not lied to him. She had told him the truth and he had refused to believe her. He had treated her with contempt and cruelty. Luke knew he would never forgive himself. When he had read about her life as a child, with her mother, Luke had felt the acid burn of tears stinging his eyes, and his anger against himself had trebled. His anger, but not his love. His love, he recognised now, had been born fully formed and complete the moment he had set eyes on her!

His love. Broodingly, Luke went towards the bed, lithe and silent as a panther as he moved through the darkness. His love was a burden he would never lay on Suzy's shoulders. His report had told him what kind of person she was: the kind of person who put others before herself, the kind of person who gave up her own future to look after the mother who had never cared enough to love and protect her as she deserved. One day Suzy would meet someone for whom she felt as he felt about her. Someone she could love as he loved her!

A savage pain tore through him. He had reached the bed and he sat down on it. Because of Suzy's nightmares he had taken to wearing a pair of boxers to bed, but he still had to turn sideways so that she wouldn't see the telltale outline of his erection.

'It's all right Suzy, I'm here,' he told her gently.

'Oh, Luke hold me, please!' Suzy begged him.

Her nightmare terrified her. In it she was trapped underground on her own. She could hear Luke talking to her, but he wasn't there with her, and she was afraid. Afraid that she would die without seeing or touching him again.

Physically she had not suffered any harm from her incarceration in the vault beneath the grotto, but emotionally and mentally it was taking her longer than she had expected to recover.

Reluctantly Luke took hold of her, tensing as she burrowed closer to him. His body registered the fact that she wasn't wearing anything other than a pair of silky briefs.

Here in Luke's arms was the only place she felt safe, Suzy acknowledged as the nightmare receded and the warmth of his body comforted her. Comforted her and then aroused her, she admitted shakily, as the familiar feelings of longing and love filled her.

Unable to stop herself she leaned forward and brushed her lips against his shoulder, and then his throat, her tongue-tip investigating the taut flesh over his Adam's apple.

Luke felt as though he had been speared by a firebolt His erection was no longer a mere outline beneath his boxers, but a hard and obvious straining of flesh, aching to be touched and tasted as she was touching and tasting his throat.

'Luke, please kiss me,' Suzy whispered against his lips.

'Suzy…'

'Please,' she begged.

'Suzy, this isn't—'

'I love you, Luke,' Suzy burst out, unable to keep her feelings to herself any longer. 'I love you and I want you. You saved my life, and in some ancient cultures when a person saves another person's life it means that that person belongs to them for ever. And I want to belong you, Luke—even if it is just for tonight.' She was speaking so quickly her words were falling over one another. She had had it all worked out, what she would say to him, but suddenly, halfway through her planned speech, her courage began to desert her. 'You are my soul mate, Luke,' she whispered.

Everything she was saying was true, but once she would never, ever have said such words—because her pride would not have allowed her to do so! Her brush with death had changed her, Suzy recognised. She was no longer afraid of being laughed at or rejected. She wanted—she needed Luke to know how she felt.

Luke tried to control what he was feeling. She didn't mean it! She might think she meant it, but she didn't. It was the trauma of what she had experienced that was making Suzy feel that she loved him. That and her belief that he had saved her life. After all, she hadn't loved him before, had she? Once she was over her trauma she would realise that she didn't love him at all.

Just because he loved her it didn't mean that he could take advantage of what she was offering right now.

'Luke…'

Her pleading whisper burned into him like fire. Her hand was touching his belly, tracing the curve of his scar. Luke felt as though he was about to explode with need and hunger.

'Luke…'

Her breath whispered past his mouth and Luke knew that he was lost. Hungrily he possessed the softness of her lips, savouring them, parting them, thrusting his tongue with hard demand into the sweetness of her mouth.

Without him knowing how it had happened his hand found her breast and cupped it, moulding it, teasing the peak to rise up into his palm as he stroked and tugged its tautness.

He wanted her.

He loved her!

Abruptly Luke reined in his feelings. He loved her and he had to protect her from her traumatised belief that she loved him.

The small whimper of distress she made as he firmly put her from him tore at his heart as nothing ever would tear at it again.

'Luke…' Suzy protested achingly. 'Please stay with me, Luke. Please…'

But he had already gone, firmly closing the door between the bedroom and the sitting room and leaving her on her own.

Suzy gave a small start, unable to believe she had slept for so long. She had originally come up to the bedroom halfway through the afternoon, intending to catch up on the sleep she had lost the previous night, lying awake and longing for Luke.

Luke! She wasn't sorry that she had told him how she felt about him. She was glad! She was proud of her love, and proud of loving him. Her brush with death had altered her attitude a great deal, she acknowledged, but it did not seem to have altered Luke's attitude towards her.

He might not love her, but he wanted her, Suzy told herself. Last night he had wanted her—even if he *had* left her.

Getting out of the bed, she went into the bathroom. She still hadn't got used to the sensuality of the room, or the open sexuality of its erotic décor. She hadn't used the huge bath as yet—which was more of a sunken pool than a mere bath—but suddenly she was tempted to try it.

Returning to the bedroom, Suzy picked up the ice bucket and the complimentary book of matches from the pretty desk. Back in the bathroom, she pushed the door closed, put down the ice bucket and then carefully lit the candles that surrounded the bath. Even their shadows seemed to cast intimate and erotic dancing images around the room, and a sensual shudder ran through her. This was dangerous. She knew it was dangerous. But still she filled the bath. The water gushing from the dolphin jets glittered against the mosaic tiles.

The circular pool was so deep that she had to walk down into it. Like a Jacuzzi, it had a ledge to sit on, and was easily large enough to accommodate two people. Two people? Her and Luke? Suzy scooped up a handful of blue-green bath crystals from the jar beside her. As she dropped them into the water it turned a deep cloudy aquamarine before slowly clearing to the colour of the purest sea water. Self indulgently she lay back in it, floating in sumptuous, languid pleasure.

Worriedly Luke opened the bedroom door. It had been Lucy who had told him that Suzy had felt tired after lunch and had gone to lie down. A doctor had checked her over after her ordeal, and had pronounced her fine, but what if he was wrong—what if he had missed something?

And where was Suzy now? Not in either the suite's sitting room or the bed. Had she got up and gone back outside to join the children by the swimming pool?

It had been a long day—he had been cooped up in his office all morning, rearranging security for the President Njambla's visit because he had not been happy with it after all. He felt hot and tired and in need of a shower.

Unfastening his shirt, he removed it. In the mirror he could just see the tip of the small, still livid scar that disappeared below the belt of his chinos. The scar Suzy had touched and kissed.

Luke dropped the shirt and rubbed his hand across his forehead and then his eyes. He had to put Suzy first, not himself! But he couldn't stop thinking about how she had touched him last night in bed, how she had told him that she loved him! Irritated with himself, he stripped off the rest of his clothes. Somehow Suzy had got under his skin in a way that no other woman ever had—under his skin and into his heart. Just thinking about

her brought a familiar ache to his body—a
fiercely elemental and dangerous ache!

He opened the bathroom door and strode
in. And stopped. And stared. He cursed under
his breath, because his body was way ahead
of him, in reacting to what he could see, and
there wasn't a damn thing he could do about
it other than make a grab for a towel.

What the hell was Suzy doing anyway?
Just lying there, so that from where he was
standing he could see quite plainly every silk-
skinned inch of her. She hadn't seen him yet,
though. She was facing away from him, and
the steam from the water had made her hair
curl wildly.

The scent of the candles she had lit filled
his nostrils. Heat, need, hunger poured
through him in an unstoppable torrent, filling
every nerve-ending.

The towel slid from his fingers as he advanced towards the tub.

The candlelight seemed to highlight the
sexuality of the wall frieze, and Suzy stared
at it, lost in her own private Luke-filled fan-

tasy. If Luke was with her now... A liquid ache of longing curled up through her body. And then she blinked as suddenly she saw that he was actually standing in front of her.

Pleasure touched her every nerve. She gave him a blissful, adoring smile and murmured his name on a happy sigh before asking curiously, 'Is that really physically possible?'

As Luke looked up and saw what she was studying a hard burn of colour ran up under his skin. That round-eyed look of innocence she was giving him was destroying him—and his self-control! He looked at the frieze again, and then back at her, where she lay floating in the bath, surrounded by the candles. His gut twisted as he saw the wet tangle of curls between her thighs and the dark peaks of her nipples.

Ignoring her, he headed for the shower.

Suzy could hear its noisy water running and her face burned as she wondered what on earth had possessed her to make such an idiotic remark.

Luke turned off the shower. It had been a wasted exercise, since it had cooled neither his emotions nor his arousal. Padding naked back to the tub, he demanded grimly, 'Do you want me to tell you if it's possible—or do you want me to show you?'

'Luke!' Suzy turned over too quickly and choked on a mouthful of water as Luke stepped down into the tub beside her.

He was crazy for doing this. Luke knew that. And even more crazy about the woman who was staring at him, her huge eyes already darkened with smoky, sensual arousal and excitement.

'Which one do you want to try first?' Suzy heard Luke whisper in her ear as he nibbled deliciously on the lobe and stroked a wet fingertip along her collarbone, and down to the valley between her breasts, and then along the upper curve, seeking out the wet thrust of her nipple where it surged above the water in excited eagerness for his touch.

'Mmm... Well?' Luke was demanding.

She gave a shocked gasp, her thoughts scattering like raindrops as Luke sank beneath the water, only the top of his head visible, his hair seal-dark and wet. His mouth was cool and firm as he took captive the nipple he had previously claimed, and the sensation of her body floating in the water, Luke's head between her breasts, his mouth on her nipple, his hand moving determinedly between her thighs was too much for Suzy's self-control.

The water in the tub might be cooling, but the wetness inside her certainly wasn't. She could feel its heat spreading through her as Luke's fingers found her—found her and touched her, stroked her, opened her...

She was beyond reason, beyond reality—beyond anything but this. The stroke of his hand, the suckle of his mouth, the soft rhythmic sensation of the water...

She could feel the surge of her orgasm beginning to mount, as unstemmable as the tide itself, and, as though Luke could feel it too, he picked her up and carried her towards the steps.

The thud of his own arousal beat through his body and echoed in his ears. This wasn't need, and it wasn't desire. It went way, way above and beyond that, and it had taken him to a place where he was a stranger, a humble acolyte, only just beginning to learn the true meaning of the new world he had entered.

As he carried her up the steps to the floor, Suzy could see their reflections in the mirror. Water ran from their bodies and her nipples, swollen from his caresses, peaked dark and hard in the candlelit room.

'Which position do you want to try first?' he asked again.

Luke had placed her on a pile of soft towels and was leaning over her. Excitement, shock and disbelief ran through her veins like liquid fire. Her body ached heavily with unsatisfied need, and Suzy knew she didn't care how he completed their union just so long as he did. She was in physical pain with her desire to have him inside her, her emotions and her body coiled to breaking point.

'This one?' His voice was a dark, tormenting whisper against the back of her neck as he moved her.

Shudders ran through her body as his hands stroked the skin of her bowed back. In the mirror she could see him leaning over her, his erection straining from the silky mat of hair surrounding its base.

'Is this what you want?' he whispered dangerously.

His hands were on her hips, and as she tilted her head back to look above the mirror and over their reflections she could see the position he was mimicking on the wall above them.

Violent shudders convulsed her.

'Or would you prefer this one?'

Suzy had to grit her teeth to prevent herself from crying out for him to stop tormenting her as he moved her again. Her body seemed to have no means of moving by itself. It had become completely obedient to his touch, whilst deep inside her the tension continued to grow so that she felt as though at any second it would spill from her and flood through her.

Her gaze embraced his erection with a molten look of longing and hunger. She reached out and touched him, hot flesh beneath her shaking fingertips, stretched over him, the foreskin pushed back to expose the rounded tip, dark and rosy. She rimmed her fingertip around it feeling his whole body jerk.

Luke could feel himself starting to shudder as his control collapsed in on itself. Her touch was destroying everything he had put up against her. He had become a mindless physical instrument, reliant on her touch, dependent on her response.

He could feel the onset of his orgasm. From a distance he could hear her moaning his name, pleading with him to fill her with his body.

They were still lying on the towels together, and Luke was holding her, lifting her, entering her only just in time. On a surging explosion of relief and release his one powerful thrust carried them to completion on fierce, unending surges of pleasure that racked them again and again whilst he spilled hotly into the waiting, wanting heat of her body.

They were only just in time for dinner. Suzy was pale and lost in her own private bliss-filled world. Her mouth was swollen, but nowhere near as swollen as her breasts and nipples, which she had thankfully been able to conceal beneath her clothes. Her eyes looked slumberous, and somehow sensuously knowing.

As they reached the drawing room door she drew back a little unsteadily to look up at Luke, her gaze filled with so much emotion it hurt Luke to look back at her.

It wasn't real, he told himself grimly. She just *thought* she loved him. He had had no right to do what he had just done, and one day she was going hate him for it!

As he already hated himself!

He could feel Suzy quivering at his side. He looked at her again. Her face was pale, her eyes luminous, her mouth… Luke could feel his own pupils dilating in response to the message of those swollen lips. Inside his head he could see, feel, taste the more intimate flesh their swollen softness mimicked.

To his disbelief, Luke realised he had an erection.

'You go in,' he told Suzy curtly. 'I've got something I need to do.'

Oblivious to the real meaning of his words, Suzy tried to calm herself as he walked away from her, leaving her to enter the room alone.

Immediately Lucy and Charlie bounded over to her side. They were lovely children, she acknowledged tenderly, and they deserved to have a woman in their lives who truly loved them.

As he stood in his office and willed his erection to subside Luke knew that he could not allow the situation to continue. For Suzy's sake. If he allowed her to stay on at the villa now he knew he didn't have a hope of keeping out of her bed...their bed.

Right now she believed she loved him, but Luke knew that she did not. He had to send her away!

CHAPTER THIRTEEN

Suzy stared out of the salon window. She felt heavy-eyed from another night of too much thinking. And she had no idea where Luke had spent the night—it certainly hadn't been with her, in the suite!

The salon door opened and she spun round quickly, but it was Lucy.

'Are you waiting for Luke?' she asked Suzy. 'He's with Daddy. I wish you were going to be with us always, Suzy,' Lucy burst out, and then blushed. 'Some of the girls at school have got stepmothers and they say that they don't like them, but I think it would be cool if we had one—especially if she was like you.'

Suzy couldn't stop herself from giving the girl a fierce hug. She was still holding her when the door opened and Luke walked in. He had been avoiding her since they had made love in the bathroom, and Suzy knew it was only Lucy's presence that prevented her from begging him to tell her why.

'I wish that you were my stepmother, Suzy,' Lucy said passionately, hugging her tightly.

Luke frowned when he heard Lucy's outburst. It was no secret to him that Peter Verey was attracted to Suzy—what sane man would not be? He had had to fight off his own jealousy every evening since Suzy had been at the villa as he'd watched the other man flirting with her, but now it was surging almost out of control, forcing him to turn on his heel and stride out of the room.

Suzy watched him go, confusion filling her. What had caused him to suddenly walk away.

'So, it looks as though the President isn't going to show, then?' Sir Peter questioned.

'I'm afraid that it does look very much like that,' Luke agreed grimly as they stood together in his office. 'We've spoken to his people, and reiterated to them just how important this discussion is, but apparently he feels that he would be too exposed if he comes to Europe.' Luke's mouth compressed. 'He's playing with us, of course. We all know that. But there's nothing we can do other than wait. There's a rumour that he needs to be at home at the moment to quell some potential unrest. If that's true it could be several months before he's ready to set up fresh talks.'

'It looks like we've dragged you out here for nothing, Luke,' Sir Peter apologised.

Luke remained silent. After Sir Peter had left, he typed out a report and made several telephone calls. He had e-mails to answer and a variety of other correspondence to deal with...

It was late afternoon before Luke saw Suzy again. She was playing with the children, oblivious to the fact that he was watching her with a hungry lover's gaze. Right now he wanted nothing more than to take her in his arms and take her to bed, make her tell him how much she loved him.

But he wasn't going to it. No he was going to send her away.

Suzy looked up as she saw Luke approaching them Her skin was glazed with perspiration and her hair was sticking in exercise-dampened curls to her neck and face. She had enjoyed herself with the children, but Luke had never been out of her thoughts. Automatically she went towards him, and then stopped as he stepped back from her.

'You shouldn't be out here overdoing things.' His voice was clipped, and Suzy stifled her dangerous need to believe that he was speaking so because he cared.

'I'm fully recovered now,' she told him valiantly.

'Good, I'm glad to hear it.' He paused and looked at her, and something went still and cold inside Suzy's heart. 'Sir Peter's meeting with President Njambla has been cancelled,' Luke went on, in the clipped voice. 'I've booked you on to a flight for London mid-morning tomorrow.'

'What? No—Luke…' Suzy started to protest, but he was already walking away from her, leaving her white faced and desolate as she struggled to contain her pain.

She was still aching with misery a couple of hours later, when she went back to the suite to pack her clothes and have a shower.

For some reason she couldn't explain, even to herself, she did something she had never done the whole time she had been staying at the villa—and that was to turn the key in the outer door to the suite, locking herself inside and Luke outside! Out of temptation's way!

Her packing finished, she went to shower, determinedly refusing to look at the tub as she walked past it on her way back to the bedroom, before tiredly wrapping herself in a towel and crawling onto the bed.

Luke frowned as he turned the handle of the suite and realised the door was locked.

Wryly he wondered if Suzy had the least idea of what his Army training had equipped him for, and several seconds later he opened the door with silent ease.

She was lying on the bed, curled up on her side with her back towards him, quite obviously asleep.

Stripping off, he headed for the shower. He had a busy night ahead of him, sorting out the chaos caused by the African President's machinations, and he had come up to the room to grab a power-nap first.

Half an hour later he was to all intents and purposes still fast asleep on the sofa in the sitting room when he heard it. The smallest of muffled sounds. But he was awake immediately and on his feet in one smooth, predatory move.

Suzy was still asleep—but no longer peacefully. Her hands were clenched and she was moving frantically in panic. She gave a small, shrill whimper of terror. She was having her nightmare again!

Luke reached out and touched her bare shoulder.

Immediately she screamed, and then woke up. She sat up, shivering as she wrapped her arms around her knees, oblivious to her own nudity.

'Luke!' Suzy's eyes rounded, her gaze flickering towards the door to the sitting room. 'How...? What are you doing in here?' she demanded.

'It's our room,' Like reminded her calmly.

'Our room?' Suzy looked bravely at him. 'But you don't want me here.'

She was starting to tremble, and Luke had to grit his teeth to stop himself from reaching out and taking her in his arms.

'Why don't you try and go back to sleep?' he suggested.

It would certainly suit him if she did, and it would suit him even more if she covered herself up. Right now just the knowledge that he had only to turn his head and he would be able to see the silky curve of her naked shoulder, the small hollow at the base of her throat which he had already explored so thoroughly, was driving him crazy.

'No!'

The vehemence of her denial made him freeze.

'No. I can't go back to sleep. I'm afraid that I'll start dreaming again about the grotto,' she whispered.

Like her, Luke must have showered, she recognised, because he was wearing a towel wrapped around his hips so low that she could see the beginnings of his scar. Automatically she reached out and touched it with her fingers, and then with her lips. He stood at the side of the bed as immobile as a statue.

What was she doing? Was she going crazy? Suzy didn't know and she didn't care. She was high on the scent and the taste of Luke, drugged by her own need for him.

Luke tried to resist, to remind himself that it was for her own sake that he was sending her away, but his body overruled him. One minute he was telling himself he wouldn't touch her, the next she was in his arms and he was kissing her as though he was starving for the taste and feel of her!

Kissing her was like tasting a freshly picked peach—each taste made him eager for another, and then another, so that he could posses her unique sweet juiciness for ever...

Suzy pulled away from Luke's kiss to press her lips to his throat, and then his chest, stroking her fingertips through the soft warmth of his body hair as just for this moment she allowed herself to pretend that Luke was really hers, that she had rights of territorial possession over his body—it was hers to do with as she wished, to enjoy as she wanted, to touch, explore and know in a hundred different ways, so that she could store that knowledge for her future enjoyment.

Her tongue-tip rimmed his navel and felt the fierce clench of his muscles. She lifted her head and looked sideways at the purple scar, and she reached out to touch it again, liquid emotion shining in her eyes. A badge of courage and more importantly—to her, at least—a badge of love for his fellow human beings.

She bent her head, her lips poised to breathe a tender kiss against it. But Luke's harsh objection savaged the silence, and suddenly she was rolled underneath him, pinned there by the hard weight of his body whilst he stilled her soft sounds of pleasure with the savage heat of his mouth.

She shouldn't be doing this, Suzy knew. Luke did not love her as she did him. But how could she stop? How could she resist the need that was filling her, overruling reason and pride? She loved him! She wanted him! And right now nothing else mattered other than that he was holding her.

As his hands sculpted Suzy's body Luke told himself that it was for the last time. He cupped her breasts, savouring the malleability of them. He wanted to kiss them, lick them, pleasure them until she arched under him and writhed against him in hungry need. He wanted...

'No!'

Abruptly he released Suzy and stood up, his back to her as he stared out of the window.

Suzy waited, whilst her heart jerked in pain, and then, when he didn't move, she picked up her towel, wrapped it around herself and walked silently into the bathroom so that she could cry her eyes out under cover of the noise of the running shower.

Oh, why hadn't she stopped him before he had rejected her?

Outside in the bedroom Luke touched the scar on his side. She had touched it, kissed it, looked at him with luminous loving eyes.

She *didn't* love him, he reminded himself. She just thought she did. She just believed she did because she thought he had saved her life! If she did love him she would have known it before that time in the grotto, just as he had known he loved her.

But love could grow, Luke told himself fiercely. And if Suzy believed that she loved him then who was to say that she might not in time—?

No, Luke told himself savagely. No. He would not do that to her. He would not lock her into a relationship that denied her the right to love freely. He could not.

He could not bear to let her go—but he had to for her own sake!

The first thing Suzy saw when she woke up was the small package on the bedside table. Picking it up, she opened it. Inside was her passport and her flight ticket, plus a generous amount of euros.

Tears filled her eyes as she carefully removed the money and put it down on the bedside table.

She had breakfast in her room—though there was no need for her to feel so anxious, she assured herself miserably. Luke wasn't likely to come in and say goodbye, so there was no risk of her flinging herself into his arms and telling him how much she loved him, begging him to give her a chance.

A chance? Did she really think there was one after the way he had rejected her last night—even though his body had wanted her? That could only mean that he didn't love her. She knew that!

There was nothing for her to linger for. She had already said her goodbyes to the children, and to Sir Peter, and given him her thanks for their hospitality.

'Will you come and see us at school?' Lucy had begged Suzy, tears in her eyes as she hugged her fiercely.

'Of course I will,' Suzy had assured her.

Poor little scraps! They had so much in material terms, and yet so very little in all the ways that mattered.

She stayed upstairs until she saw the taxi arriving from her bedroom window, and then she went down, carrying her small case with her.

The children were waiting to wave her off, wearing the clothes they had bought together. Suzy had to blink away tears as she hugged them and promised again to keep in touch.

Unable to stop herself, she looked towards the closed door to Luke's office, willing him to come out. But to what purpose? The only thing she really wanted him to say was, Please don't go! followed by, I love you! And she was not likely to hear him say those words, was she? Forcing a wan smile, Suzy gave the children one last kiss and then walked out to her taxi.

Standing in front of the window of his small office, Luke watched her. He had been deliberately avoiding her—why make problems for himself? Why put himself in a situation he already knew he couldn't fully control? She was opening the taxi door. By the time he took one deep breath and counted to ten she would be gone.

One deep breath…

He flung open the door to his office and raced towards the front door. He had almost reached it when Sir Peter suddenly emerged from his own office and called out urgently to him, 'Luke—quick! I need you. The Prime Minister's on the phone, Njambla's people have been back in touch. The meeting's on again.'

For a second Luke was tempted to ignore him—breaking one of his own unbreakable rules—but he could hear the taxi door closing, and his conscience was telling him that he had to let her go. His face stripped of expression, he turned away from the front door and walked towards Sir Peter.

CHAPTER FOURTEEN

Suzy had read the breaking story about a certain African President's meeting in Italy over her breakfast, not long after her departure from the villa—the same morning, in fact, as the post had brought her another letter advising her that regretfully its senders could not offer her a job with them.

Following her return home, she had written to every library and organisation she could think of, determined to pursue her dream of finding work as a trainee archivist. But it was a narrow field, with very few vacancies.

'You mustn't give up,' Kate had told her firmly.

'I don't want to,' Suzy had admitted. 'But it's not an easy market to break into, and at my age—'

'Your age?' Kate had shaken her head chidingly. 'For heaven's sake, Suzy, you aren't old!'

'I'm not twenty-one, and just down from university,' Suzy had reminded her ruefully. 'Potential employers want to know what I've been doing for the last few years, and why I didn't finish my degree first time round.'

'What? You were nursing your mother,' Kate had defended indignantly.

'And then there's the fact that I left the magazine—and I don't have any references from them.'

'They were subjecting you to sexual harassment,' Kate had argued, but Suzy had been able to see from her friend's expression that Kate knew that things did not look good for her.

'Still, there is somewhere I can get a job,' Suzy had told Kate cheerfully.

'Yes—with us,' Kate had replied promptly.

Even though she was grateful to her friend, Suzy had shaken her head. 'No, Kate. You know that I won't take charity,' she had told her gently. 'I was referring to the supermarket—I've worked there before.'

'Suzy, you don't need to do that!' Kate had protested. 'You know we'd love to have you working for us.'

'Kate, you told me yourself only last week that you were struggling to find enough work for the part-time girl you've already got,' Suzy reminded her. 'No. The supermarket will be fine!' she had told her, and she had meant it.

She felt very guilty about the fact that she had said nothing to Kate about either Luke or her time at the villa. But somehow she had just not been able to bring herself to do so...

'I hate this job. I've only been working here a week and it feels like for ever. And as for that supervisor—she's more like a prison warden!'

Suzy smiled sympathetically at the pouting teenage girl sitting grumpily at the till next to her own.

'It's okay once you get used to it,' she assured her, whilst privately acknowledging that she could understand her dislike of their supervisor, whom Suzy thought was a bit of a bully.

The supervisor apart, though, Suzy quite enjoyed working on the supermarket check-out— After nearly three months she actually had her own regular customers, who favoured her till—old ladies, in the main, who were lonely and appreciated the fact that Suzy did not rush them and had time to listen to them.

The bullying supervisor didn't approve. She constantly hectored Suzy about the time she spent listening, complaining that Suzy wasn't pulling her weight because she wasn't dealing with as many customers as some of the other girls. She had urged Suzy to discourage them.

'But they're lonely,' Suzy had protested.

'So what? We aren't here to provide them with someone to talk to!' the supervisor had told Suzy angrily. 'And it's not as though they spend very much. Just a few bits and pieces, that's all.'

'They like coming in because they can go to the coffee shop,' Suzy had responded. But her defence of her elderly customers had only infuriated the supervisor all the more.

'Yes, and they'll go in there and sit all day if they can, just drinking one cup of tea!' she had snorted grimly.

Suzy tried not to think about her supervisor. She needed this job because she needed the money. They had had a good summer, so at least she hadn't had to spend money keeping the flat heated. Every penny counted now—she had even thought of applying to the council for an allotment. Fresh air and fresh food would be good for her—

She checked her thoughts and she looked down at the small bulge of her stomach. To say that it had been a shock to discover that she was pregnant was more than an understatement!

Of course the discovery of her pregnancy had meant that she'd had to come clean to Kate about Luke, and although she had been surprised, her friend was being wonderfully supportive.

Luke's baby!

A soft absorbed look filled Suzy's eyes followed by a flash of fiery maternal protectiveness. Unlike her own mother, she was not going to bring her baby up in an atmosphere of misery and complaint. But if her baby was a girl, Suzy had decided she would warn her against falling for a man like her father!

Her doctor had assured her that everything was fine and normal—single motherhood didn't raise any eyebrows or comments any more—and now that she had got used to the fact that she was pregnant Suzy was thrilled and excited. But not as thrilled and excited as she would have been if she had been sharing things with Luke—a Luke who loved her...

Now she was entering fantasyland, she derided herself. And what was more she was demeaning herself by even thinking about wanting to have him love her.

There was a lot of commotion and noise coming from the supervisor's office, which was behind her and several yards away, and in front of her at the checkout a young mother with a screaming toddler was struggling to unload her trolley.

Suzy smiled sympathetically, unable to stop herself from mentally fast-forwarding to the arrival of her baby. Money would be very tight, but she was determined that somehow she would manage.

There was still a lot of noise coming from behind her. She could hear the supervisor's voice raised in protest, and she could hear a man. A man? That was *Luke's* voice—she was sure of it.

Luke had had enough.

The last fourteen weeks had been the longest of his life. First he had told himself that he was a man of honour, and that as such he was honour-bound to leave Suzy to make a life for herself without him. Then he had told himself that it was only natural that he should check up on her to make sure she was okay after what she had been through.

Then he had admitted that if he *did* check up on her he was going find it damned hard to walk away—especially if she was still under the delusion that she loved him. And then finally he had admitted that there was no way he could live without her and that he had to see her again!

He had finished the contract he'd been working on, handed over his active role in their shared business to his partner, and announced that from now on he was going to be running the small estate he had inherited.

A hiccup in the children's recovery and their return to their homeland had added to the delay, making it fourteen weeks instead of the fourteen days he would have preferred before he was finally free to seek Suzy out.

When he had called round at her flat the woman who had the apartment below hers had informed him that she was at work. It had taken him an hour and a good deal of patience and flattery before she had finally given him the information that Suzy was working in a supermarket.

He had wasted another hour driving through the traffic to find it, and now this shrill-voiced woman was telling him that it was impossible for her to take Suzy off the till she was operating, and that if he wanted to see her he would have to wait until her shift was over.

Luke wasn't prepared to wait a single minute longer—not after having waited nearly four months—and so, ignoring the supervisor, he strode towards Suzy.

'Luke!' Suzy wasn't even aware that she had spoken his name, never mind stood up, to stare in disbelief as Luke strode towards her.

Then he stopped, his gaze going from her face to her body. He couldn't possibly tell, Suzy assured herself frantically. She was barely showing. Her bump was still relatively small. Even so her hand crept protectively towards it as she tried to cover it from him.

Shock and awe! Where had he heard those words before? Luke wondered, dazed. Certainly not in connection with what he was feeling right now. Suzy was pregnant! Suzy was having his baby!

Whilst the young mother watched in fascinated interest, Luke shifted his gaze from Suzy's stomach to her face.

'Go and get your things,' he commanded brusquely.

'My things?' Suzy gulped. 'What? I—'

'We're leaving—and now!' Luke told her fiercely.

Suzy told herself that she should refuse to have anything to do with him, but instead she heard herself protesting shakily, 'Luke, I can't just leave. I'm working. There's no reason—'

'There's every reason,' Luke corrected her savagely.

And before Suzy could stop him he had reached for her and placed his hand where hers had been, flat and hard against her belly, where his child was growing.

'There's this, for starters,' he told her thickly. 'My child. And if that isn't enough…'

Suddenly Suzy was conscious of the silence surrounding them. The curious looks of the customers and the angry face of her supervisor.

'If you leave this till now you will be in breach of your employment terms and your job could be at risk,' the supervisor was intoning.

'She'll be handing in her notice anyway,' Luke answered coldly.

Handing in her notice? Suzy glared at him.

'You can't say that!' she hissed, as Luke put his hand beneath her elbow and almost frogmarched her away from the till. 'I need this job, Luke.'

'What you need and what I need are not my prime concerns right now,' Luke told her flatly. 'Our child's needs are.'

He shouldn't be feeling like this, Luke told himself. He shouldn't be feeling triumphant, exuberant, delighted that the child Suzy was carrying—his child—meant that he had a logical and undeniable reason for forcing his way into her life. But he was!

Our child! Suzy could have wept.

Outside in the car park he bundled her into a large four-wheel drive vehicle and then got in himself. It was nearly four months since she had seen him. And he hadn't even looked at her properly, never mind attempted to touch her…kiss her…

'I've just got back from seeing the children,' Luke said to her. 'They're well enough to receive treatment from a hospital in their own country now, and their aunt has officially taken charge of them.'

'Oh, Luke, that's such good news,' Suzy responded in delight.

'Yes, it is,' he agreed quietly. 'Suzy, why didn't you let me know about the baby?'

'Let you know?' she stared at him. 'I…'

How could she tell him that she hadn't wanted him to feel responsible, that she hadn't wanted him to feel that she had deliberately allowed herself to become pregnant in order to trap him. He already knew how much she loved him, and she imagined that in a man's eyes a woman who became pregnant with his child after he had rejected her had to be doing so in order to force his hand.

She didn't feel she could tell him any of that, so instead, she simply said huskily, 'I...I just didn't think that it was necessary.'

Luke felt the pain of her words explode inside him.

'I heard from Peter the other day. He mentioned that you've kept in touch with the children,' he announced abruptly.

'Yes...yes, I have,' Suzy agreed. 'I feel so sorry for them. They need a woman in their lives who loves them. A stepmother, perhaps.'

As she spoke Suzy was thinking of the young woman Lucy had written to her about—the daughter of some older friends of Peter's who had taken quite an interest in Lucy and Charlie.

'Thinking of applying for the job yourself, are you?' Luke demanded harshly.

Suzy stared at him, his words coming as a shock after her own private thoughts.

'How could I?' She asked. 'I'm pregnant with your child.'

Her answer wasn't the one Luke wanted to hear. What he wanted was to hear her telling him, as she had done before, in that soft, loving voice of hers, that she loved him and only him and that she would always do so!

'Why are you working in that supermarket?' he asked curtly.

'Because it was the only place I could get a job!' Suzy returned tartly. 'Now that I'm going to have a child to support—' She stopped and bit her lip. The last thing she wanted was for him to think she was trying to get money out of him.

'*You* are going to have a child to support?' Luke demanded as he turned the car in the direction of the motorway. 'This child is our child, Suzy, and I consider that I have as much responsibility for supporting him or her as you do—if not more.'

'Luke, where are you taking me?' Suzy asked, as she silently digested his statement.

Things were happening too fast. She was still in a state of shock. In fact she was still expecting to wake up and open her eyes and find that she had been dreaming!

'Home,' Luke replied, further astounding her.

They were heading towards the country, leaving the city behind.

'Home?' Suzy queried uncertainly. 'But...'

'Where else would I be taking you?' Luke asked. 'After all, it's where you and our child now belong!'

'I have my own home,' Suzy protested sharply. 'I have my flat.'

'You can't bring up a child up there,' Luke told her flatly. 'And you certainly will not be bringing up *my* child there.'

Suzy drew in a sharp breath of indignation. 'There is nothing wrong with my flat,' she told him. 'You have no right to do this, Luke.'

'You are carrying my baby,' Luke said harshly. 'How much more right than that do I need?'

'Maybe I am—but that doesn't mean that you can just walk into my life and...take over...or kidnap me!' Suzy wasn't far from tears of emotional reaction.

'No? I beg to differ. You see, the way I look at it, Suzy, you gave me some damn important rights when you gave yourself to me—when I gave you my child.'

Shocked into silence, Suzy leaned back in her seat and closed her eyes. She just could not believe that any of this was happening— that Luke had conducted this swift and effective campaign of repossession which had brought her totally into his power.

As she tried to fight the wave of tiredness that suddenly gripped her Luke turned off the motorway.

'It isn't very far now,' he told her. 'The estate is just the other side of the village. You'll be able to see the church spire first.'

Estate...village...church spire. Suzy's head was thumping with a reactionary headache.

They were right in the heart of the English countryside at its quaint best. Autumn might be just around the corner, but the trees were still in full summer dress—the hedges heavy with leaf, fields of crops waiting to be harvested stretching away from the road.

Suzy saw a sign, Flintock-upon-Adder, and then they were driving through a picturesque village. Its houses clustered around an immaculate green, with weeping willows dipping into the waters of a sedate river and then the road curved past a small Norman church to run alongside a stone wall. Beyond it Suzy could see a small park, and then she caught her breath at the beauty of the Queen Anne house she could just glimpse through the trees.

Luke was turning in to a tree-lined drive and the house lay in front of them.

As he brought the car to a halt outside it Suzy turned and told him determinedly, 'Luke, I want you to take me back to my own flat.'

'Not yet,' Luke refused calmly. 'Not until we've had time to talk. Come on—I'll take you in and introduce you to Mrs Mattock. She's the housekeeper—I inherited her along with the house.'

'You inherited this house?'

'Yes, from my father. It's been in the family ever since it was first built.'

Mrs Mattock was calm and welcoming, apparently not in the least bit fazed that Luke had returned with an unexpected guest.

Although she was both pleasant and discreet, Suzy suspected that the housekeeper was well aware of her pregnancy as she escorted her upstairs to a pretty guest bedroom. It was decorated in a simple and traditional style, complete with its own bathroom so that Suzy could, as the housekeeper put it, 'freshen up'.

'Mr Luke said that I was to serve tea in the library, miss,' she informed Suzy before turning to leave. 'It's the third door on your left off the hallway. A lovely room it is too. It was the old master's favourite. He would have been right pleased that Mr Luke had taken it over, that he would!'

From the window of the guest room Suzy could see the house's lovely English country garden, and the church just visible through the greenery of ancient trees.

In the bathroom, with its plain white san-itaryware, she found immaculate white guest towels and a tablet of what looked like hand-made soap. Against her will she found herself thinking what a wonderful home this house would be for a family.

A wonderful home, maybe, but never *her* home—nor her child's, she reminded herself sharply as she left the room and headed for the stairs, breathing in the soft scent of lavender and beeswax from the well-polished furniture.

Dutifully following Mrs Mattock's instruc-tions, she resisted doing more than just peep-ing inside the half-open door of what was a lovely sunny south-facing sitting room, and headed instead for the door to the library.

Outside the room she paused, reluctant to go in. But determinedly she took a deep breath, and then reached for the door handle and turned it. As she opened the door and walked in, Suzy acknowledged that the very masculine panelled room, with its impressive partners' desk, suited Luke. She could see that he felt very much at home in this lovely house. But then why shouldn't he?

'Suzy.' As he came towards her she backed away from him. 'Mrs. Mattock is going to bring us some tea,' Luke said.

'Yes. She told me,' Suzy answered curtly, wondering what on earth they were doing, exchanging such stilted small talk when they had far more important matters to discuss— like Luke's high-handed virtual abduction of her!

'Luke, you shouldn't have done this,' she said angrily. 'You have no right to—'

'To what? To be concerned about the welfare of my child and his or her mother?'

Suzy had to blink frantically to banish her threatening tears. Hormonal emotions, she told herself crossly.

'This baby I am having wasn't planned, Luke—we both know that,' she reminded him. 'He or she was…was an accident. I don't consider myself to have any claim on you—and anyway, you don't…'

'I don't what?'' Luke probed, when Suzy fell silent without finishing her sentence.

'Suzy took a deep breath. 'You don't love me!' There—she had said it! 'You don't love me. You don't even like me very much.'

'I don't love you?' Luke gave a harsh laugh.

'And why on earth did you come to the supermarket in the first place?' Suzy persisted, ignoring him.

Luke had had enough! It was hell on earth for him, having her standing there in front of him when what he wanted more than anything else was to have her in his arms—her *and* their child!

'Why did I come to the supermarket? Why do you think I came?'

Suzy's heart was beating crazily now, with a mixture of dangerous emotions.

'I don't know,' she admitted, wetting her lips nervously with the tip of her tongue. She had been so caught up in Luke's reaction to the discovery that she was pregnant that she hadn't been able to think past it and question why he had come looking for her in the first place.

'In Italy you told me that you loved me,' Luke said curtly, half turning away from her as he stood staring out of the library window.

Suzy could really feel her heart thumping now. Yes, she had told Luke that she loved him and he had shown her in no uncertain terms that he did not want that love. She had more than her own feelings to consider now. She had her child's to think of as well! No way was her child going to suffer the same unhappy childhood she had known! For her baby's sake she needed to be strong.

'I did say that, yes,' she acknowledged a little unsteadily. 'But I realise now that I—'

Idiotically she discovered that something inside her just would not let her say the words *I don't love you!*

'That you made a mistake.' Luke finished her sentence for her flatly, causing relief to surge through her as he inadvertently rescued her.

'I...'

Suzy had to bite on her lip to hold back the pain seizing her as she tried to deny her love. Something inside her was telling her that to deny her feelings was as great a betrayal of her child as humiliating herself by loving a man who did not want her.

'You didn't have to come to the supermarket to find that out, Luke,' she said instead. 'Surely the fact that I haven't made any attempt to contact you must have reassured you that I—'

'Reassured me!' The violence in Luke's voice as he swung round to confront her silenced her. 'Reassured me?' he repeated savagely. 'What the hell are you talking about, Suzy?' He broke off abruptly as there was a discreet rap on the door and Mrs Mattock came in wheeling an immaculately set tea trolley, complete with a heavy silver teapot.

'Will Ms Roberts be staying the night, Mr Luke?' she asked politely.

'Yes!'

'No!'

Locked in mutual anger, Suzy and Luke glared at one another as the housekeeper discreetly departed.

'Would you like me to pour the tea?'

As Luke nodded tersely Suzy had to quash a hysterical sound of mingled pain and disbelief. Here they were, in the middle of a situation so tense and painful that she felt faint from the stress of it, and she was pouring tea—like someone out of a Victorian novel!

But automatically she went to pick up the heavy teapot.

'Of course I realised that your belief that you loved me sprang from the trauma you'd undergone,' she could hear Luke saying tightly behind her. 'I may have realised I loved you before that event, but—'

The teapot wobbled in Suzy's hand as shock weakened her muscles. There was tea

in the cup, in the saucer, and on the immaculately starched traycloth.

'Suzy!'

Luke grabbed the heavy silver teapot with
one hand and put a steadying arm around her.

'What did you just say?' she demanded
weakly. She was shaking so much she could
hardly stand, and it was heaven to lean into
Luke's warm strength. 'Are you trying to say
that you fell in love with me before I got
trapped in the grotto?' she asked dizzily.

'Yes. Not that I wanted to admit it. I was
still labouring under a misapprehension about
you then, and whilst a part of me wanted to
be proved right about you, a much larger part
of me most certainly did not.'

Suzy was having to struggle to assimilate
what he was saying. Luke loved her? Luke
had loved her even when he had thought he
ought to hate her? Joy was beginning to well
up inside her, flooding through her veins.

'Are you feeling all right?' Luke was fuss-
ing, man-like. 'Why don't you come and sit
down?'

'No,' Suzy told him fiercely. 'No. I'm not going anywhere, and most especially not out of your arms, Luke, until you tell me exactly when you knew you loved me!'

'Exactly when?' Luke looked down into her unguarded face, and what he could see there made his heart start to sing.

'Probably the first time you kissed me,' he admitted ruefully. 'And certainly by the time you ran away from me on that hilltop and I realised that if I didn't do something you were going to hurt yourself.'

A pink blush stained Suzy's face as she remembered how he had held her, her body spread on top of his.

'When I told you I loved you, you rejected me, though,' she pointed out quietly. She could feel his chest rising and then falling with the intensity of his sigh.

'I had to, Suzy. It's well known that the kind of trauma you went through can make a person feel the strongest kind of emotion towards the people they shared it with. I knew I loved you, but I didn't want to trap you into a relationship when I was afraid that your love might not be the real thing.'

'Oh, Luke I fell in love with you the moment I set eyes on you,' Suzy told him softly. 'I looked at you and it was just as though… I looked at you and I knew you were my soul mate,' she told him huskily.

For a moment she thought he wasn't going to make any response, but then he put down the teapot and turned her gently in his arms. Placing one hand on her belly, he whispered softly, 'Sorry baby, but I think you'd better close your eyes whilst I kiss your mother!'

And then he lifted both hands to Suzy's face and, cupping it, began to kiss her with a slow, gentle passion that grew and built until they were so closely entwined that even their heartbeats matched.

'I can't begin to tell you how long these last fourteen weeks have felt,' Luke whispered achingly to her. 'First the meeting with Njambla, and then I had to persuade my partner to take over my active role in the business. Then there were problems with the children, and all the time I kept warning myself that by the time I did get to see you, you would have realised that you didn't love me after all. You don't know how many times I cursed myself for not keeping you with me when I had the chance, for not taking the love you were offering me. And then when I saw you today and I realised you were pregnant…'

She could see the pain in his eyes, as well as the love.

'I didn't want you to feel you owed me anything,' she told him quietly. 'I didn't want anything from you, Luke, that you couldn't give with love.'

'Are you sure you're feeling okay?'

'I'm fine,' Suzy reassured Luke as he led her out of the church and into the late autumn sunshine to the joyful sound of wedding bells ringing.

Her elegant cream silk dress discreetly concealed the curve of her belly, and under the benign gaze of their wedding guests Luke leaned down to kiss her.

'Who would have thought that first kiss you stole from me would lead to this?' he murmured teasingly in her ear.

Suzy laughed in real amusement. 'I may have stolen it,' she reminded him, 'but you returned it—and with interest.'

Luke laughed back, placing his hand on the curve of her belly as he did so.

A hovering photographer snapped the pose, and then the one following it, when Luke drew Suzy firmly into his arms and kissed her tenderly and thoroughly.

EPILOGUE

'LUCY looks very serious and important.' Luke smiled at Suzy as they watched Lucy, Charlie and Sir Peter, along with Anne, the young woman he had asked if he could bring with him to baby Robert's christening, getting out of their car.

'Well, being Robert's godmother is a very serious and important role for her,' Suzy told him with a smile.

Lucy had been thrilled when Suzy had asked her if she would like to be one of Robert's godmothers, along with Kate.

'Oh, Suzy, do you mean it?' she had asked, her face pink with excitement.

Suzy smiled now at the memory, shifting Robert's sturdy six-month weight in her arms as she looked at Luke.

They had had Sir Peter, Lucy and Charlie to stay with them over Christmas, and Suzy had heard a great deal then from Lucy about Anne, the young family friend who was now Sir Peter's fiancée.

'I know Lucy is perhaps a little young, but it means so much to her, Luke. She told me that she is hoping that when her father re-marries there will be babies.'

Robert's two godfathers were friends of Luke's from his Army days and, like Sir Peter and his family, they had been regular visitors over the months since Luke and Suzy's marriage.

Knowing the sad story of how Luke had lost his parents, and how lonely he had felt, had increased Suzy's determination to pro-vide their own children with the kind of warm, happy family environment neither she nor Luke had known.

When Luke had taken her hand, white-faced and worried after Robert's birth, anx-ious for her, having witnessed her labour, Suzy had smiled up at him and warned teas-ingly, 'You're going to have to get used to this, Luke, because this baby is not going to be lonely, like we were.'

A small smile touched Suzy's mouth as she remembered this and then looked down at Robert.

Some might consider it too soon, but she suspected that she was already pregnant with their second child, and had told Luke so only this morning.

'What? Already?'

'What do you mean, already?' she had teased. 'It only takes one successful attempt, as we both know.'

Luke had smiled, giving her a deeply sensual look that had made her both laugh and colour up a bit. 'Of course, if you would like to be sure...' he had said as he advanced towards her.

'Luke!' Suzy had protested as he had removed the bathrobe she had been wearing and taken her in his arms. 'Luke, we've got guests,' she had reminded him mock primly. 'And they will be waiting for their breakfast.'

'Let them wait,' he had murmured, finding the exact spot at the side of her neck where the touch of his lips always reduced her to hungry need.

'It's Robert's christening today,' she had added, several seconds later, but without any real urgency in her voice.

'Mmm...so it is,' he had replied.

If any of their guests had found it odd that they should arrive at the breakfast table rather later than planned none of them had been impolite enough to say so, but Suzy thought she had caught Sir Peter Verey's fiancée, Anne, focusing on her thoughtfully.

She liked Anne, and thought she would make Sir Peter a good wife and the children an excellent stepmother. Already she was building rapport with them, and it made Suzy smile to hear how many times Lucy mentioned her name when she was talking to her.

The sun was shining and their guests were now filing into the old church.

Robert woke up and looked around with interest.

He was very much his father's son, Suzy reflected—and not just in the way he looked. He had Luke's sometimes imperious and questioning manner, even at six months old.

As they followed their guests into the church Luke took Robert from her, cradling him expertly. And as she watched them Suzy saw father and son exchange a knowing male-to-male look.

Her heart flooded with emotion and instinctively she moved closer to Luke. She was so happy, so blessed, so loved.

Luke was her other half and she his. Deep down inside herself Suzy knew that they had been fated to meet. Fated to meet one another and fated to love one another.

They were soul mates.

In Luke's arms Robert smiled up at his father, and Suzy touched her stomach gently.